Soulless Devil

Sons of Valentino
Book 3

Kylie Kent

For Oliva Bennett
I can't wait to watch you grow up and find a Romeo of
your very own
XOXO

This book contains scenes of non-consensual and consensual sexual acts, profanity, and violence. If any of these are triggers for you, you should consider skipping this read.

This is a work of fiction. Names, characters, businesses, places, events, and incidents are either the products of the author's imagination or used in a fictitious manner. Any resemblance to actual persons, living or dead, or actual events is purely coincidental.

Chapter One

Romeo

She's here again. Sitting in the same spot. The desk piled high with open books as she relentlessly writes handwritten notes on a notepad. It's been the same for the last seven nights in a row. For hours at a time, she has people coming and going from her table. She's tutoring them.

I watch her from my little darkened corner on the top floor, looking down through the glass wall to her table beneath me. I'm pissed that I can't seem to shake this feeling. I don't even know what to call it. When I saw her seven nights ago, I thought I was having a heart attack. Pain ripped through my chest. The longer I watched her, the more that pain seemed to morph into a foreign sensation.

The overwhelming need to protect her. To make sure she's safe. To keep her.

Which is a ridiculous fucking thought. I don't keep people. Especially girls. I have my family, my mom, dad, brothers. I don't want anyone else in my life. I don't need anyone else to watch over to ensure they don't end up six feet under. I don't need more funerals to attend. This life sees enough death without adding girls like... *that* to the mix.

I've never even spoken to her. I know her name is Olivia, and I've heard people call her Livvy. And I know she's fucking smart, probably smarter than me. Which is saying something because I've never met anyone smarter than me.

Sounds conceited but it's not. It's just the truth. A fact. And you can't argue facts. They aren't biased. How do I know she's so fucking smart? I may have planted a listening device under her table. How the fuck else was I going to learn shit about her?

It's Saturday night. I should be out partying it up with my twin brother. Luca's the yin to my yang and our school's star quarterback. Unless you're family, you probably wouldn't know who's who when we're in the same room. The only identifiable difference is the ink under our shirts.

Livvy yawns and stretches her arms above her head. I need to either get out of here or man up and talk to her. I've never found it hard to approach girls. Usually, I can just point and curl my finger, call them over to me. Again, not conceited when it's been proven time and time again and the outcomes are always in my favor.

However, something tells me that's not going to work for Little Miss Prim-and-Proper down there. I know I should walk away. It's the right thing to do. She wears fucking cardigans and skirts down to her knees. Her strawberry blonde hair is always tied up in a mess, piled on top of her head, often with a pencil in it.

I've never been good at doing the right thing, which is exactly why I find myself strolling out to the café and ordering her a caramel latte. Her drink of choice. Those listening devices are worth every cent. Just as I'm walking back into the library, my phone rings, blaring out "Hey Brother" from its speakers.

"Shit, sorry." I offer the librarian currently glaring at me a polite smile before stalking back outside and answering the call. "Luc, this better be important. I'm busy," I tell him.

"It is important. I need you to meet me at the gym. There's a fight starting in twenty," he says.

We've been running our own little lucrative fighting club for the past six months. It started out as us simply organizing others to fight. But that got old really quick, and Luca stepped into the cage. We've all had intense lessons from our Uncle Bray, who was an undefeated underground fighter in his heyday. We've both also been trained in every form of combat you can think of.

Our father, the current Don of the Valentino Crime Family, insisted we knew how to protect ourselves using our bare hands. That relying on guns, knives, was how people in our world got themselves an early ticket to hell. He's not wrong. I've seen more than my fair share of fallen men. Some I knew well, while others I didn't even know their names. Just that they were part of the famiglia.

"What the fuck, Luc? You weren't supposed to be fighting this weekend," I remind him.

"Yeah, well, plans changed. Are you coming or not?" he asks, as if it's a legitimate question. One thing I would never do is leave any of my brothers hanging. Especially Luc. He's my twin. We share a bond I don't have with the older two, Theo and Matteo. We're all close, but it's different with Luc.

"Of course I'll be there, but don't expect me to have a fucking smile on."

"The day you smile, Romeo, is the day I'll run for the hills, because I know hell will be freezing over." He laughs. "See you soon, bro." The call disconnects before I can say anything else.

Walking back into the library, I head to the cranky

old bat sitting at the front desk, the one glaring at me like I have two heads. "Evening, ma'am. I was wondering if you could deliver this to Livvy. She's sitting on the second floor with a huge stack of law books in front of her."

"I know who Livvy is, young man, but I'm not your delivery person. Go give it to her yourself." She dismisses me with a wave of her irritated hand.

"Look, I would... but my brother just called. There's been a family emergency. My sister was in an accident, and I need to head to the hospital. Livvy looked really tired, and I thought she could use this to get her through the rest of the night." The lie slips from my tongue so easily. I don't have a sister, but this lady doesn't know that.

I mean, my older brother's best friend, Savvy, is the closest thing to a sister I could ever have but she isn't blood. She's always been there growing up. She comes to every family event. And I'm almost certain that one day she'll be my sister for real. If Matteo could chain her down, he would. In a heartbeat.

"Fine, but this is a one off thing. I don't have time to be chasing after all of you." The woman huffs as she takes the cup.

I look at her name badge. "Thank you so much, Margaret. I really appreciate it, ma'am." The smile I offer her, the one that usually gets me anything I want, has absolutely no effect whatsoever. She sends me a final glare as she walks off with the cup in hand. Turning around, I head back out of the library.

I swear to God, Luc is going to owe me for tonight's missed opportunity.

I pull up to the industrial garage we've converted into a club. It's already packed. Vehicles everywhere. Thankfully, I don't have to teach any motherfucker a lesson for parking in my spot.

Jumping out of the car, I'm greeted with enthusiasm from the crowds of college assholes hanging around in clusters. I nod to acknowledge them, but that's all they'll get from me. They aren't my friends. They're a means to fund this club. That's all. I don't have friends. I've never needed them. I have Luc and Luc has friends. He's always been the popular one. I'm just his weird lookalike, who tags along with him everywhere. At least that's how we're perceived.

Entering the garage, I find my twin enjoying the attention of a busty brunette. I roll my eyes, walk right up to them, and pull her off his lap. She shrieks as I place her feet on the ground. I'm gentle. It's not like I'm out to hurt the girl.

"Go find another dick to ride," I tell her, gesturing in the opposite direction.

Luc smirks up at me. "What the fuck, bro? I was enjoying that."

I stare at him for a moment. He's lying. He wasn't enjoying her attention. He was just taking it. "Sure you were. Get up. You wanna fight? Let's do this shit and get it over with. Some of us have shit to do tonight."

He stands, pulls his shirt over his head, and kicks his shoes off, leaving himself in a pair of black jeans. "Really? What were you doing?" he asks.

"I was studying. You know, that thing people do at college," I tell him.

Luc laughs—more like howls. "Please, you've never needed to study a day in your life, Einstein."

"Well, there's always a first for everything."

He shrugs a shoulder. "Fine, don't tell me what you were really up to. I'll find out anyway," he says as he shakes his arms out and stretches them above his head. "Let's do this." He smiles.

My brother doesn't fight for the money, obviously. He lives on the adrenaline, the high, the pain of each blow. He loves to play with his opponent, with the crowd. No one ever knows if he's going to win or not. Until he decides to throw that knockout blow. The one that's endgame for his opponent and has left him undefeated.

"Okay, boys and girls, let's get this party started!" Luc yells over the roar of the crowd as he enters the ring.

I take my place standing at the door of the cage. If I think for one minute he's in any kind of real danger, I will be at his side in seconds, blowing someone's head off.

Everyone cheers as my twin jogs around the platform, putting on one hell of a performance. The theatrics have the crowd throwing bets either for or against him, though the majority are counting on Luc for the win. I look over to Henry, the little math geek who's been our bookie since we started. He sends me a thumbs-up. It's a good night. Lucrative.

The opponent enters the ring, giving me a wide berth. I smirk at him. *It's not me you should be avoiding. You're about to get in a locked cage with a Valentino.*

He's either stupid, brave, or both. I don't give a shit which. Regardless, it's his funeral. Not literally. Hopefully... We've been lucky so far. No deaths on our hands—due to cage fighting anyway—and I'd like to keep it that way.

The fight starts and I watch as Luc takes hit after hit, doing nothing to block the blows coming at him. I feel each one, like they're connecting with me. My blood boils, and my hands clench to get in that ring and strangle the motherfucker dumb enough to hit my brother. I don't though. I know this is part of the game that Luc insists on playing.

Eventually, after a few minutes, Luc shakes his arms out before tilting his head to one side, his glare aimed at his opponent. I can't hear what they're saying.

However, judging by the look on Luc's face, it's not fucking good.

My brother throws a punch to the guy's head and the crowd goes silent as we watch his body fall to the ground. Luc then kicks his motionless form in the ribs, probably cracking a few before storming out of the cage, through the crowd. That's not like him, usually when he knocks someone out, he'll stick around until they come to.

I follow my twin out to the parking lot. "Luc, hold up." I pull him around to face me. "What the fuck was that?" I ask.

"A fight."

"What'd he say to you?" I try again.

"He said he'd bet my mother would put up more of a fight than I could," he hisses. "Then he went on to say that he intended to find out firsthand."

"What the fuck." I storm back into the garage. "Everyone get the fuck out now!" I yell at the gathering crowd. They don't argue. It takes less than five minutes to clear the garage and empty the lot. When everyone's gone, I look over to Henry. "You're going to want to finish that later," I tell him.

"Sure thing, boss." He stands, leaving all the money, books, and everything else spread out on the table.

The guy who just signed his death warrant is starting to come to as he groans, trying to pull himself up from the floor. I walk up to the cage and throw the lock on the door. He's not leaving this garage. Not in one piece at least. Luc walks back inside, pressing the button on the wall, and the doors close. "What's the plan?" he smiles at me.

"I don't know. Think we should just hand him over to Pops? Let him deal with the little fucker who threatened his wife? It's never ended well for anyone who's tried before." I laugh, thinking of just how much fun Pops would have ripping the fucker limb from limb. There's a reason my father is one of the most feared bosses in New York.

"We could, but then we'd have to explain why I was fighting him in the first place," Luc says.

"Right, and then we'd miss out on all the fun." Bending down, I pull the knife from the holster strapped around my ankle.

"We're not doing this here. I don't feel like cleaning it up. Get him in the trunk." Luc disengages the cage door and enters. Kicking the guy in the head before he walks around him, he grabs a leg and starts dragging the fucker out.

I open the door and pop the back of Luc's Escalade open. Pulling out some zip ties, I wrench the fucker's hands and feet together before I help Luc throw him into the car.

"Usual spot?" I ask him.

"Yep."

"Let's go." I jump into the passenger's seat. This night is not going how I wanted it to at all. I should be at the library. I should be getting to know Livvy. Not in a car, about to kill some bastard whose name I don't even know.

That's my life for you, though. When you're born a mafia prince, you don't get to live free and wild. You don't get to do as you please. From a very young age, we're trained in the art of war. We're told not to take threats lightly, to protect the family at all costs. And when someone threatens my mother, you better believe I'll put that threat to bed real fucking fast.

Chapter Two

Livvy

I bring the cup to my mouth. Nothing comes out. Damn it, I was enjoying that latte. I wish I knew who sent it over to me. I'd really love to thank them. It's only a *little* freaky that whoever it was knew exactly what kind of coffee I drank.

It must have been Sandra, my roommate and best friend. She hates that I'm always studying until the library forces me out when they close. I don't have the luxuries in life that she does though. I wasn't born with a trust fund big enough to buy an island. She says it doesn't make us any different, that my middle-class upbringing is something she envies. I didn't have a bad childhood. My parents loved each other; they love me and my sister. We had what I guess you'd call the typical American family. My dad was a police officer, my mom a teacher, and I grew up in a picturesque town in Georgia. Everyone in Covington knew everyone. Which is why, when it came time to apply for colleges, I aimed for the ones farthest away.

New York was my dream and now I'm living it. Well, I'm living it from the table. In the library. At college. But when this is all over, when I graduate, that's when I'm going to become one of the many lawyers who hustle and bustle within the city that never sleeps. I've been here just over a year, and I still haven't ventured far into the city. I work, study, eat, and repeat. I don't have time for much else. But that's okay because this is a marathon. Not a race.

I pull my phone out and send Sandra a message.

ME:

Thanks for the coffee. It's just what I needed.

She texts me back.

SANDRA:

What coffee?

I snap a picture of the cup and send it to her.

ME:

Did you send me this?

Sandra:

Nope, wasn't me. Sorry.

Well shit, if it wasn't her, who could it be?

I decide to call it a night. The library is due to shut in thirty minutes anyway. I pack all my stuff into my shoulder bag, smile, and wave at Margaret as I pass her at the exit. Then I turn back around. "Ah, Margaret, that coffee you brought me earlier... Do you know who it was from? I'd like to thank them."

"Some young man. He didn't leave his name. Sorry, Livvy," she says.

"Oh, okay, thank you." Maybe it was one of the guys I tutor. I'll ask them when I see them throughout the week. I tutor a total of ten people: four girls, six guys. It's a way to make a little extra money while adding to my college extracurriculars.

I pull my jacket tight around me as I make the short walk to my dorm building. The hairs on the back of my neck prick up while that sensation like I'm being watched washes over me. I've had it every night this week, but tonight it's different. I don't know what it is, but it's more of a creepy feeling than before. It's probably just the mysterious coffee and not knowing who sent it that has me more on edge.

My steps quicken and my hand wraps around the bottle of mace in my bag. My dad insisted on me carrying it everywhere. The minute I step through the door of my building, I sigh in relief. I turn around and stare out into the darkness but I can't see anyone. Walking up the three flights of stairs, because my step count is the only form of exercise my body gets, I finally arrive at my room. My hands shake a little as I pull my keys out and unlock the door.

Something really did spook me tonight. I've always been one to rely on my gut, and tonight I had that feeling of danger. Growing up with a police officer for a dad, my sister and I were well aware of all the horror stories; we heard them nightly. I'm sure my dad was trying to scare us into never putting ourselves in situations that could be threatening. Like walking alone at night. Or keeping a tight schedule that never changes. Which is exactly what I've been doing.

I might need to study in here for a little while. Change my routine up a bit. Argh, I love the library. It's my happy place, so I decide I'm not giving that up. I'll just leave earlier or find someone to walk home with. I think my imagination is overactive right now. I need to find a way to tune it out. Something to block the sound of my father's voice screaming 'I told you so' over and over again in the back of my mind.

Ten minutes into watching some crappy reality show about southern belles on my laptop, Sandra bursts through the door. "You're back? Did you find your mysterious coffee donor?" She waggles her eyebrows up and down.

"No, Margaret at the library just said it was a *young man*," I tell her.

"I think you've gone and got yourself a little admirer, Livvy. I'm not surprised though. I mean, if I were into girls, I'd do you." She shrugs.

"Ah, thanks?"

"You're welcome. So, who have you met lately? Who could it be?"

"I have no idea. But don't you think it's a little creepy that whoever it was knew exactly what kind of coffee I drank?"

"It could have been a lucky guess. Or they've seen you order it?" she suggests.

"I also think I was followed on the way home tonight. I had that feeling of being watched."

"You need to stop walking home so late by yourself. Call me next time and I'll walk with you." She lies flat on her bed on the opposite side of the room. She doesn't have to cram into this tiny shared dorm room with me. She can afford an off-campus apartment but she insists on having as normal a college experience as

16

Thanks for reaching out. I can offer you a trial session to see if we work well together. How's Tuesday at two p.m.?

Kind regards,
   Livvy

His response comes minutes later. I don't know why I'm getting butterflies in my stomach at the thought of reading it. This is not a normal reaction to an email. I've had emails from students enquiring about tutoring often enough to not get nervous over them. Yet, as I read his subject line—entitled *extremely grateful*—I can't help the weird smile that appears across my face. I click open.

Dear Livvy,

Tuesday at two p.m. is perfect. Some would say it's fate that I'm as free as a bird at that exact time. I look forward to meeting you then. Name the place and I'll be there.

. . .

Yours,
   Romeo Valentino

Again with the *yours*? I shake my head. What that means is beyond me right now.

"What has you smiling like you just got your hands on your favorite cookie?" Sandra asks from across the room.

"Huh? Nothing," I lie, ignoring her as I hit reply.

Hi Romeo,

I'm not so sure about fate, but let's meet in the library. Second level. I usually occupy a table towards the back of the law section.

Regards,
   Livvy

Just as I hit send, Sandra pops up next to me on my bed, her eyes directed over my shoulder. She gasps out loud. "Hold up! How the hell do you know Romeo Valentino?" she shrieks.

"I don't know him. He wants to book tutoring sessions," I tell her. Sandra scoffs, like that's something unbelievable. "What?" I ask her. "Do you know him?"

"Not really, but I've heard of him." She doesn't look at me as she answers the question. I don't know what she's hiding but it's definitely something.

Chapter Three

Romeo

I've been counting down the hours for the last few days, just holding out. Waiting for Tuesday at two p.m. to roll around.

I watch Livvy check her watch for the tenth time in the last five minutes, from my spot at the back of the room. It's five till two. I still have five minutes to stand and watch her. Something that is fast-becoming my favorite pastime. She's nervous about something. The way she keeps tightening the ponytail that sits on top of her head tells me as much. Which is also something different, as her long strawberry blonde hair hangs down her back. I've never seen it in anything other than the messy bunch of hair she usually has piled on top of her head.

Did she do this for me? That thought clenches my gut with an awful feeling. *Does she know who I am? Is that why she's nervous?* Of course, she would have Googled me. What girl meets up with a complete stranger without looking them up first? Fuck, I'm an idiot for using my own name.

She's not going to want to tutor me if she knows. Either that, or I had pegged her all wrong and she's just like every other girl on this campus who thinks they want to be the next mafia wife.

But that can't be right. She's way too fucking sweet and innocent to want that.

Kicking off the wall, I make my way towards her, sitting in the seat opposite her at the table. She looks up at me with wide eyes. Wide, bright-blue eyes that I let myself drown in momentarily. Before I offer her my trademark Valentino smile. "Hi, I'm Romeo." I hold my hand out for her to shake.

She hesitates briefly before placing a palm in mine, and I swear I have the urge to never let go. "Livvy, thanks for meeting me here." She smiles shyly before pulling her hand away and looking down at the table.

"No problem, although I'm the one that should be thanking you. You'll really be helping me out here."

"Right, so let's start by you telling me what you're struggling with?" she suggests.

I'm guessing the honest answer of 'trying to keep my cock under control around you' isn't what she wants to hear. "English Lit is kicking my ass this semester," I lie. I don't even take English Lit.

"So, you're an English Lit major?" she asks with raised brows.

I tilt my head at her. "Is that hard to believe?" I fire back.

"Not at all. I just figured you're more suited to being on screen than behind the lines." She blushes a lovely shade of red.

I smirk. "Are you objectifying me within minutes of meeting me, Livvy?" I ask her.

"What? Oh my god, no! I'm so sorry! I didn't mean..." She shakes her head vehemently, her eyes wider than a deer caught in headlights.

"It's okay if you are. I don't mind." I wink.

"Well, I'm not. I was making a sound observation. That's all."

"An observation about my looks. Correct me if I'm wrong, but the very definition of sexual objectification is treating someone as an object of desire."

Her eyes somehow widen a bit more, though I didn't think it possible, and it's hard not to laugh at her obvious distress. "No, that's not what I meant. I'm sorry if I offended you."

"You didn't," I tell her.

"Okay... how about we start over and you tell me what you need me to help with specifically, and I can tell you if I can assist you or not."

"You can," I assure her. I'm not about to let her pull out of this little arrangement.

"I think I'm a better judge of that."

"Right. English Lit, it's the classics, but it's Austen I connect with the least."

"Okay, do you have your class outline? I can take a look at it."

"Ah, shit, I knew I forgot something," I stumble out. *How did I not think to get a fucking outline?*

"It's fine. You can email me a copy later. What's your latest assignment about?"

"The theme of marriage in Jane Austen's *Pride And Prejudice*," I tell her something I did look up before I came today. "Which, if you ask me, is fucking stupid. The whole 'women must marry a rich man to be fulfilled thing.' It's fucked up."

"It was a vastly different era, Romeo. You're looking at it from a twenty-first century point of view. Try to imagine what it was like for women in the time of Austen. They didn't have the freedoms we do today. All they had was marriage. It was what secured them a good life, or damned them to one filled with unimaginable hardships."

I tilt my head at her again. This time with curiosity. I knew she was smart, but I didn't know I'd be hanging on every word that left her mouth. "What are your views on marriage? It's no secret that most girls here are looking to nab their first husbands."

"If I ever get married, he won't be just my first husband. He will be my only one."

"Interesting."

"What's interesting about wanting a life partner?" she counters.

"It's interesting that people still dream of happily ever afters, especially someone as intelligent as you are. You have to know they only exist in fairy tales," I tell her.

"Are you the product of divorce or something? Are your parents unhappy?" she asks, scrunching up her face as if the thought tastes sour on her tongue.

"No, my parents are happily married, but they're the exception. Not the rule," I admit. Perhaps she didn't look me up. Because if she had, she'd know exactly who my parents are. "What about you? Were you the product of divorce and that's why you dream of something different?"

"Nope, my parents are soul mates. They met in college and have been together, happily, ever since."

"What do they do?" I have this need to know everything about her.

"My dad's a retired police officer, and my mom's a teacher," she says.

25

My back straightens. Her dad's a cop? Or a retired cop... I knew she was too good to be true. There's no way I can drag the daughter of a cop into my life.

"What do your parents do?" Her question is the same one I asked, except it's not something I'm at liberty to tell her.

"My dad's an entrepreneur, and my mom was a teacher before she married my dad. Now, she's practically his under—*business partner*, I guess you could say." Fuck me, I almost said *underboss*. It's something my brothers and I joke about often. There is nothing that happens in our family that my mom doesn't know about. I really need to get away from this girl. I can't think straight. If I could bring myself to stand up and walk away, I fucking would. I can't though. It's like she's trapped me in her orbit. Blinded me with her brightness.

"So, do you plan to be the eternal bachelor then? If you don't believe in soul mates? Marriage?"

"I believe in what's in front of my eyes," I tell her. And I believe I might have just stumbled upon the one girl who was meant for me. It's a cruel fucking joke. To send me the perfect girl and make sure she's the same one I can't fucking have.

"And what's that?" she asks.

"I believe that you are the answer to my dreams, Livvy." My eyes drop to her chest as her breath hitches. "I believe you're going to make sure I pass this assignment with flying colors," I add on.

Livvy clears her throat. "Right... I, ah, I'll have a look tonight and email you a study plan. That's if you want to continue sessions with me...?"

"Why the fuck wouldn't I?"

"I'm not sure? Some people, a lot of people, don't really gel well with me. It's okay if you don't. I can recommend other tutors."

My gaze peers into hers. "Those people who don't *gel well* with you are fucking idiots, Livvy, and you're far better off without them." I mean every word I tell her.

She lifts one shoulder in a half shrug. "I'm used to it. It's okay. So, what's your schedule like? I'm free on Tuesdays, same time, and Thursdays and Friday nights."

"I'll take all of them."

"Really, you want three sessions a week?"

"I need a lot of help." I smirk.

"Okay, well, how about we meet back here Thursday at six thirty?" she suggests.

Two days away. I have to wait two days to see her again. Well, to talk to her anyway. "That's fine. I'll see you here."

"Okay, I'll email you later tonight or tomorrow morning with some things for you to look up and consider."

"Sure, sounds good."

"Thank you." She stands when I do.

I give Livvy a small wave rather than pull her into

27

my arms and kiss the fucking life out of her like I want to. Cold showers are going to become my friend.

Chapter Four

Livvy

I left the library early tonight. I still felt like I was being watched, but it wasn't the same as a few nights ago when it made my skin crawl. My phone rings as I'm walking home. I glance at the screen. It's my parents.

"Hey," I answer.

"Hey, honey. How's life in the Big Smoke? Ready to come home yet?" my dad asks.

"Ah, not yet. College is good, and New York is good. It's not half as bad as you think it is," I tease.

"No, it's worse. Listen, I got a call from an old buddy of mine who's working out of the Manhattan district."

"Dad, stop. Whatever crime statistics you're going to use to try to scare me into coming home, I don't want to hear them."

"Livvy, this is serious. You need to be careful. Where are you right now?"

"I'm walking back to my dorm room," I tell him, rolling my eyes.

"From where?"

"From the library. It's literally a five-minute walk, Dad. I'm fine. How are Mom and Skylah?" Asking about my mom and little sister usually gets him off my case.

"They're good, safe here in Covington," he groans.

"Dad, I promise, if I thought I wasn't safe, I would run right home."

"Okay, maybe I can come out to New York and visit for a while."

"And where would you stay? In my dorm room? I don't think my roommate would appreciate it, Dad."

"Yeah, you're probably right." He sighs.

"I love you, Dad. I gotta go. I'm about to enter the elevator and the signal cuts out." I press the button on the panel. I'm forgoing the stairs tonight.

"Okay, sweetie. Your mom says hi and sends her love."

"Right back at ya. Bye, Dad." I hang up without waiting for his reply. I love my parents but, god, they can be overbearing at times. Okay, *most* times. They're suffocatingly loving. Which I know isn't a bad thing. It's just that I'm not a child anymore. I'm not sure they're ever going to accept that fact.

"You're early," Sandra says as I walk through the door.

"I am." I smile.

"Good, I'm hungry. Dump your bags. We're going out to eat. My treat." She stands and looks me up and down. "Right after you change."

"What's wrong with what I'm wearing?" I ask. I actually made extra effort today. I put on a nicer skirt and blouse and even flat-ironed my hair.

"Nothing, when you're sitting in the library." Sandra walks over to her wardrobe. "Here, wear this." She tosses a black dress my way.

"I can't wear your clothes. I'm fine in what I'm wearing," I tell her.

"You can and you will. Please... for me?" she asks, with a pout *and* while batting her eyelashes.

"You're not going to give up, are you?" I sigh, holding out the tiny black dress.

"Nope, besides, I've been dying to go out with you."

"When you say *out*, what exactly do you mean?" I ask.

"Dinner, and maybe some drinks," she says.

"I'm not twenty-one. I can't drink," I remind her. Neither is she, but that doesn't ever stop her.

"Rules are made to be broken, babycakes." She winks at me.

"Rules are set to make us safe," I fire back. I have no intention of drinking tonight. I will, however, go to eat, because I'm starving and my package of chicken-flavored ramen isn't looking that attractive right now.

"Okay, whatever. You don't have to drink. But we are dancing."

"I can't dance," I tell her.

Sandra shakes her head at me and points to the bathroom door. "Stop stalling and go change."

Following her directions, I head into the bathroom and jump in the shower quickly. I avoid getting my hair wet, because I don't have time to dry it. Also, I spent an hour in here with the flat iron this morning. I'm not wasting that by getting my hair wet again.

It isn't long before I'm walking out of the bathroom while pulling at the hem of the dress. Sandra and I might be the same size, but her style is vastly different from mine. Where I'm all conservative and like to keep things covered, she's more the *if you've got it, flaunt it* type. Which I adore. For her. Not for me. All I want to do is add a few more inches of fabric to the bottom.

"I knew that dress would look better on you. Here." Sandra reaches up and pulls the tie out of my hair. The strands fall down over my shoulders. "Perfect. Let's go."

I slide my feet into a pair of black ballet flats, and then let Sandra pull me out the door. "Wait, I forgot a coat," I tell her, tugging on my arm that's still in her grasp.

"You won't need one. It's not even cold out."

"It might get cold," I argue.

"It won't. Come on, we're going to be late. I got us a reservation."

"Okay, but if I catch a cold, you're nursing me back to health."

"Deal."

* * *

Fifteen minutes later, I'm following Sandra through a swanky, packed restaurant. "It's Tuesday night. Why are so many people here on a weekday?" I ask. Back in Covington, everyone only ever went out on Fridays and Saturdays.

"It's always busy here. That's how you know the food is to die for." Sandra smirks.

"Here you go, Miss Frendato." The waitress who led us to our table gestures towards our seats.

Just looking around has me feeling anxious. This isn't the kind of place I could ever afford and I'm feeling awfully guilty that I'm going to let my friend pay for me.

"It's fine. Trust me. Relax, Livvy." Sandra grips my hand from across the table.

As I reach for the menu, a bottle of champagne and an ice bucket is placed in front of us. "Ma'am, this is from a gentleman who wishes to remain anonymous. Enjoy." The waiter fills two glasses before tucking the bottle back into the ice bucket.

"Who would send you champagne?" I ask Sandra, pushing my glass towards her. I have no intention of drinking it. Instead, I pick up my water and take a sip.

"Not me, I believe this was sent for you." She smiles.

I scoff. "Highly unlikely." I grab the menu and read through it. There are no prices. I don't even know how to order the cheapest item.

"I'm going to do the crab cakes. What are you feeling?" Sandra asks me.

"Um, I'm not that hungry. I'll just have the Greek salad."

"That's a side dish." Sandra scowls at me. "I know what you're doing. And I'm telling you if you don't order properly, I'm going to order for you and you might not like my choice."

"Fine, I'll have the crab cakes too." I drop my menu on the table. "Thank you."

"Anytime. You know I'd do anything for you, right? If you ever need anything, all you have to do is ask."

"I know, and I appreciate that."

"So, tell me all about your session with the infamous Romeo Valentino. How stupid is he?" Her eyes twinkle with mischief.

"First of all, he's not stupid. I actually think he's way more intelligent than he was letting on. Second, it was fine. No different from any other tutoring session."

"Really? No different, even though the man is hot as Hades?"

"What? I didn't notice," I lie. Of course I noticed how good looking he was. I basically objectified him to his face. Tall. Like really tall. Well over six foot. With broad shoulders that were tightly wrapped by a black short-sleeve t-shirt. And that ass... I may have stared a little longer than is appropriate when he walked away.

"You're blushing." Sandra points at my face.

"Nope, not at all."

"Yes, you are. It's okay to think he's hot. The whole female population on campus talks about him. The guy's like the Loch Ness Monster. Everyone wants to catch a glimpse, get him for themselves, but no one can ever seem to lock him down."

"You do know he's a person, right? Not an object," I defend him. "Besides, who wants to be locked down at our age?"

"To a Valentino? Everyone, apart from you it seems."

"What does that mean? A Valentino?"

"Nothing. The family's just filthy rich. That's all."

"A majority of our classmates come from money, including you," I point out.

"I guess." Sandra picks up my champagne flute and drinks the contents in one go before refilling both glasses.

"I'm just going to go to the bathroom. Which way are they?" I ask, looking around the packed dining room.

"Down that way, to your left."

"Won't be long." I stand and walk in the direction Sandra pointed. Just as I turn the corner, taking the left she indicated, I run smack-bang into a wide chest.

My hands come up, gripping on to the person's shirt in an attempt to stop myself from falling, while a pair of arms wraps around my waist, holding me still. Looking up, I stare into the same face I sat across from today. Except it's not the same. My eyebrows draw down in confusion. I don't know who this man is, but he's not Romeo. Although he looks a lot like him. The same, in fact.

"That's not the expression girls usually have when they're in my arms," the guy says.

The voice, the accent, it's uncannily similar. I'm so confused. "I'm so sorry. I wasn't watching where I was going. And you, you just look like someone I know. Well, not know, but kind of met."

His arms are still around me. I push back on his chest to create space between us. He lets his hands fall from my waist and takes a step to the side. "And who is it that I remind you of? That you know but don't really know?"

Is he laughing at me? I can't tell. This is why I hate social situations. I can never read people right. Maybe he is the same guy, Romeo, but now he's not acting. Maybe this is the real him. "Ah, Romeo, just someone I'm tutoring. Excuse me. Again, I'm really sorry for running into you." I go to step around him and he steps in front of me, blocking my way down the hall. The hairs on the back of my neck rise. But when I look up at his face, he's not angry. I don't feel threatened by him, more... *annoyed*.

"I'm sorry. Did you say you're tutoring Romeo? And also, how do you know I'm not him?"

"I don't know how I know. I just do," I tell him. I keep the part about how he didn't come off like a conceited jerk to myself.

"But you're tutoring Romeo? A guy who's the mirror image of this?" He circles his own face.

"Well, he's a little more good looking, but, yeah." I shrug, shocking myself with my current ability to talk back.

"You're funny... and cute." His eyes travel up and down the length of me, and I suddenly feel more vulnerable.

"Luca, what the fuck is taking you so long?" Another voice comes from behind us, a voice that somehow relaxes me while it also lights up my every damn nerve ending.

"Oh, I just made a new friend, bro. You should come meet her. This is..." Luca—Romeo called him *Luca*, so I'm going to assume that's his name—points at me, as if waiting for me to fill in the blank.

I don't. Instead, I step to the side and walk around him. Stopping only when that voice calls out to me. "Livvy?"

Turning around, I smile and wave. "Hey, sorry. I gotta go." I spin and practically run into the ladies room.

Splashing water on my face and wrists, I try to calm my heart. Why does he have this effect on me? I don't understand it. I've never had a reaction like this to anyone. Not even Kirk—my boyfriend for three years in high school—could make my body react like this.

I wait for what seems like a safe amount of time for the hallway to be cleared. However, I quickly realize I didn't wait long enough once I push through the door. Leaning against the wall across from me is Romeo. He's alone, staring right at me, with an unreadable expression on his face.

Chapter Five

Romeo

I almost hit my own brother. When he blocked her path, I saw fucking red. The hardest part was... I couldn't let on how much he was pissing me off, so I pretended to not know what he was doing in this hallway.

I was watching her from the minute she walked in with Sandra fucking Frendato. My eyes were glued to her. Questions of how she knows Sandra run through my mind. Sandra's father is an associate of the family. She knows everything there is to know about the Valentinos.

What has she told Livvy? I doubt she'd be stupid enough to tell her anything. As much of a spoiled princess Sandra is, she's not stupid.

Luca walked past with a smirk and a knowing look when Livvy hightailed it into the bathroom. I shouldn't have called out to her. I don't know what the fuck possessed me to do it. I guess I wanted to make sure she knew that whatever Luca had said to her, it wasn't me. I know my brother can be an ass—to be fair, I'm usually ten times more of one. But I don't want Livvy to see that side of me. It's fucking hard to understand. Which just frustrates me more, because I've never had trouble figuring anything or anyone out before.

Livvy exits the bathroom and freezes as she stares back at me. She looks to her left and right, then back to me. "Did your stunt double leave?"

I smirk, almost smile, at her unexpected joke. "I'm sorry for whatever my brother said to you. I just wanted you to know that he wasn't me."

"I knew he wasn't you. I'm not an idiot," she says.

"Well, most people can't tell us apart." I lift one shoulder up, trying not to jump around like I just found a unicorn. She could tell...

That means something, right?

God, someone shoot me. I sound like an annoying-as-fuck lovesick fool, even to myself. Not love. I'm not in love. Lust, definitely lust. Because just looking at her in that skimpy little black dress has my cock rock-hard. I want to push her back into that bathroom, hold her up against the wall, and sink my cock into her. At the same time, I want to take my jacket off and cover her the fuck up. Why is she wearing that? It's not her usual style.

"Right, well, I better get back," she says.

"Okay..." I watch her walk away, my hands clenching into fists at my sides. Every ounce of my being forces me to let her go.

Why the fuck is this so hard?

I stalk back out and take my seat at the bar next to Luca. This restaurant is one of ours—well, our parents' anyway. It's also really close to campus, which is why we meet up here often.

"Where'd your friend go?" Luca says, making a point to look behind me.

I glare at him, silently telling him to drop it. We don't have to speak to communicate. We each just know what the other is thinking.

He holds up his hands in surrender. "Fine, I won't mention her. Just so you know, I went and asked Sandra what her plans were for tonight. She's heading to Grayson's after dinner."

"Why the fuck would I care where Sandra goes?" I ask him.

"Because she's taking her hot little friend with her." He waggles his eyebrows up and down.

"Call her hot again and I will fucking stitch your lips together," I hiss at him.

"Okay, but tell me one thing..."

I raise a brow at him, bringing the tumbler of whiskey to my lips.

"Why the fuck do you have a tutor? Are you struggling with the smarts?" he whispers like it's a controversy.

"No, idiot. She's tutoring me in English Lit."

"You don't even take English Lit," he balks.

"Which is why I need tutoring. Drop it, Luca." I down the rest of my glass, slamming it on the table when I'm done. Thirty minutes later, I watch Sandra and Livvy walk out of the restaurant. Standing, I pull Luca out of his chair. "Let's go," I grunt.

"Where are we going?"

"Grayson's," I tell him.

Like fuck am I about to let Sandra take sweet little Livvy to a dirty fucking club filled with perverts. I know the type who frequent Grayson's, because *I'm the fucking type.*

We arrive at the club and head straight up the VIP stairs. I know exactly where Sandra will be. She's always in the same booth, the one reserved for Grayson's friends and family. The owner being her brother puts her in the latter category. I find her there with Livvy, except they're not alone. There are four guys in the booth with them. Livvy looks uncomfortable as fuck. She's shrinking into herself, stuck between

41

an about-to-be-dead motherfucker and the wall. She's trapped with no way to move or escape if she wants to.

Fuck that. I storm up to the booth. "Get the fuck out of here. Now!" I grunt.

"Oh shit, Romeo, calm down, man. This is not the place," Luca whispers from behind me.

I don't pay him any attention. "Did I fucking stutter?" I look at all four guys. Their faces pale as they scamper out of the booth, doing their best to avoid any contact with me.

I glare at Sandra, who just smirks at me. "Luca, you let the hound out of the cage again, I see." She laughs.

"Every pet needs an outing every now and then, Sandy. You know that." Luca goes to slide into the seat next to Livvy. Grabbing him by the shirt, I pull him back and shove him towards the other side.

Ignoring the crap Sandra and Luca are bantering about, I turn my focus on Livvy. She doesn't look so good. "Are you okay?" I question. She's fucking pale.

"I'm fine. I just... I don't feel great. Is it hot in here?" she asks, looking around.

"How much have you had to drink?"

She didn't touch a drop of the champagne I sent over in the restaurant. And she's clutching a water bottle in her hand, the lid tossed in front of her on the table. "I haven't. I don't drink. I'm not old enough yet," she says so fucking innocently. Luca snorts and Sandra shoves an elbow into his ribs.

"How much has she had to drink?" I ask Sandra.

42

"She hasn't, swear it. She's been drinking water all night," Sandra says with a shrug.

"Why is the room spinning?" Livvy asks me. "Romeo?"

"Yeah?"

"You're my favorite tragic love," she says, and I know something's not right. Even if her words speak true to my heart... If I let myself love her, fuck anyone, it will only end in tragedy.

"Luca, call the doc, get the car, and meet us out back," I tell him. "Livvy, I'm taking you home."

"Wait... what? Why?" Sandra says, with genuine concern for her friend.

"If she hasn't been drinking, then she's either taken something or been roofied. I want the name of the asshole who was sitting next to her, Sandra."

Her face pales as she nods. "I'll text it to you. Is... is she going to be okay?"

"Yes," I say with more force than I meant to. Because there is no other fucking option. Luca is on his phone as he shifts out of the booth.

"I'm coming." Sandra jumps up to follow us.

I don't acknowledge her. Instead, I scoop Livvy into my arms. "Why are you carrying me?" She looks up at me. "Why is the room spinning?" Then her eyes widen. "Romeo, what's happening to me?"

Her panic pierces my fucking soul. "Livvy, did you take anything? Any pills or anything?" I'm certain the answer is no, but I ask anyway.

43

"No."

"I think someone put something in your drink. I have a doctor coming to my place to check you out. You're going to be fine," I tell her.

"Thank you." She leans her head against my chest. "My dad was right," she whispers.

"About what?"

"That there are some shady-ass people in New York," she says. "His words, not mine."

"Yeah, he's right about that." I leave out the part about *me* being one of them. Although, New York is about to have one less fucking predator in its midst.

By the time we make it back to our apartment, Livvy is passed out in my arms. My fingers hover over her pulse on her neck, making sure it's still detectable. Stabilized. My own heart might be running overtime at the moment. But hers is a calm, even beat. I walk up the stairs to my bedroom and place her on my bed.

"The doc's here," Luca says from my doorway.

I nod my head. The doctor enters the room and looks from me to Livvy's unconscious form in front of me. "I don't know what the asshole gave her, but she hasn't been drinking and doesn't take drugs. Find out what it was," I tell him.

"Sure, how long has she been out of it?" he asks as he lifts her wrist to check her pulse, and his eyes flick to his watch as he keeps time.

"About twenty minutes," I tell him.

"She's a lucky girl that you noticed," he says, retrieving a syringe from his bag.

I don't answer. I watch silently as he preps the inside of her elbow with an alcohol swab, secures the elastic torniquet, preps the needle, and draws her blood into the plastic tube. Once he's finished, I ask the question I've been trying not to think about. "Is she going to be okay?"

"She'll be fine. My guess would be that she's been slipped some Rohypnol. She'll have a killer headache when she wakes tomorrow. But I'll get these samples back to the lab and make sure that's all it was. Her vitals are good."

"Thanks. Send me the test results. Is there anything else I need to know? Anything I need to do?" I ask as I look down at her.

"Just keep an eye on her. If anything changes, take her to the ER. But, otherwise, just wait for her to wake up on her own."

"Okay."

The doctor leaves and I pull up a single-seat sofa that looks directly at my bed. Minutes later, Luca walks into the room with a tumbler of whiskey, which he passes to me. I take it and set it on the coffee table.

"Is she okay?"

"Doc seems to think so," I tell him. I trust Doc. He's been in our family since I can remember.

"Are you okay?" Luca asks.

"I want their fucking heads. Whoever the fuck

drugged her, I want their fucking head on a spike," I tell him, my voice calm, even.

"I'll make sure they're ready for you," he says, walking out of the room. And I know, within hours, he'll have whomever it was chained up in one of our warehouses. Usually, it's our brother Matteo who gets his hands dirty with this sort of shit. But this time, I'm going to have my own fun making this fucker bleed.

Chapter Six

Livvy

My head hurts. I had migraines when I was younger, but this is so much worse. My eyes slowly open. The room is pitch-black with a sliver of light coming from under a door. This isn't my room.

Fuck. I bolt upright. My whole body rejects the movement. "Argh, god." My stomach turns as I feel bile rise to my throat. My eyes are wide as I look around the space. I have no idea where I am. I have no idea how I even got here.

"Shit. Livvy, it's okay. Come on." Someone picks me up and carries me across the room. No, not someone, *Romeo*. He sets me down on my feet in a bathroom, and within seconds, I'm bending over the toilet bowl hurling my guts up.

"Oh god, kill me now," I groan between bouts of vomit.

Romeo kneels down next to me, holding my hair back. "You're going to be okay. The doc said it was Rohypnol. This will pass."

I stare at him as he pulls his phone out of his pocket and puts it to his ear.

"Yeah, bring a bottle of water and some aspirin." He hangs up the phone.

"I'm so sorry. Wait... I was drugged?" I ask as the brain fog starts to subside.

"Yes," Romeo grits out between clenched teeth.

"By who?"

"You don't remember being at the club with your roommate? You were sitting next to some fucker. I could tell something wasn't right with you so I brought you here and had a doctor come check you out."

I blink at him. *He did all that for me? A girl he only just met.* "Why?" I ask the same question I'm thinking.

"What do you mean why? I wasn't about to leave you passed out in a club, Livvy," he grunts.

"Oh." That's all I manage to say. Another silhouette fills the doorway, and I remember seeing this photocopy of Romeo at the restaurant. "Where's Sandra?" I ask.

"She's downstairs, sleeping on the sofa. She wouldn't leave without you," the photocopy says, handing me a bottle of water.

"Thanks." I take it and set it down beside me.

Romeo picks up the bottle, twists off the cap, and hands it back to me. "You need to drink this," he grunts —*he seems to do that a lot*.

"Here, aspirin," the photocopy says, handing Romeo a little bottle before he turns and walks out the door.

"What's your brother's name? I figure I can't just refer to him as *the photocopy* forever." I thought I knew his name last night but now I can't remember. "Not that I plan to impose on you again," I attempt to clarify. "Oh god, I should go home. I'm so sorry you had to look after me."

"Stop. You're not going home yet. I'm gonna get the doctor back here to check you over again. His name's Luca, by the way, but feel free to call him the photocopy or the stunt double."

"You don't have to do that. Really, house calls are expensive. I can just visit the clinic on campus later if I don't feel better."

"It's too late. He's already on his way," Romeo says. "Take these, have a shower, and I'll leave you some clean clothes on the bed."

I look at him and then around the room. He wants me to shower? Here. In this bathroom?

"I don't mind helping, you know. If you need help showering?" He smirks.

"Nope, I'm good. Thank you," I rush out, feeling the heat creep up my neck and face. The picture of Romeo helping me shower, both of us naked, plays through my mind.

"Okay, I'll be downstairs, but just yell out if you need anything."

"Thank you." I let him pull me to my feet. His hands linger on mine for a beat before he lets go and walks out of the bathroom, gently closing the door behind him.

As soon as the door shuts, I lean against the wall. What the hell have I done? I'm never going out to a club again. My head throbs, my whole body aches, and I just threw up in front of the hottest guy who's ever spoken to me.

Way to go, Livvy.

I wouldn't be surprised if he cancels our tutoring sessions now. Oh shit, I was supposed to email him some things to read up on last night. I planned to do it when I got home after dinner.

Turning the shower on, I wait for the room to steam before I strip off last night's dress and panties and step under the spray. I let the hot water wash over me. It feels good on my sore muscles. Picking up the bodywash bottle, I pop the lid open and inhale. It smells like him. Romeo. The citrus scent does seem to have an odd calming effect on me. Not wanting to overstay my welcome any more than I already have, I rinse off and jump out, wrapping a huge fluffy black towel around my body.

Walking back into the bedroom, I find the clothes that Romeo left on the bed. I bring the Columbia sweatshirt to my nose. I really need to stop this newfound obsession with smelling the guy. I throw on the sweatshirt, forgoing the boxers that are also on the bed. The shirt hangs down long enough to be a dress anyway. Picking up my clothes from the bathroom floor, I head out of his room and down the staircase. My hands shake with nerves.

What the hell do I say? *Thanks for holding my hair back while I disgustingly vomited everywhere. Thanks for letting me sleep in your bed?*

Which brings me to my next thought... *Where the hell did he sleep?*

By the time I make it to the bottom of the stairs, Romeo's brother is waiting for me. "Luca, right? Thank you for letting me stay here. I'm really sorry for any inconvenience I've caused." I can't seem to make eye contact with him. My hands clench around the fabric of last night's dress, which has my panties securely scrunched inside it.

"You're not an inconvenience. How are you feeling?" he asks.

"I've been better," I admit shyly.

"I bet. Come on, Romeo's cooking you breakfast."

"What? Why?" I blurt out.

"Good question—probably one you should ask him, though." Luca smirks as he turns around.

I follow him into a small dining room. Sandra is sitting at the table; she jumps up when she sees me. "Oh my God, Livvy, I'm so sorry. I didn't know. Are you okay?" she presses, as her arms wrap around me.

"It's okay. I'm fine," I tell her.

Sandra releases me, her eyes roaming over my body. "Are you sure?"

"Yes. Can we just go home now?" I ask her quietly.

"Good luck with getting lover boy over there to let you leave," she whispers back.

My eyes follow the direction she gestured with a dip of her head. Romeo is in the kitchen serving up four plates of food. He looks up and his eyes pierce mine. He finishes what he's doing and carries two dishes over to the table. "Come on, you need to eat. The doc will be here soon," he says, nodding his head to the chair he's now holding out.

"Um, you really didn't have to do all this," I say, sitting down.

"Just eat, Livvy. It's only food. Don't overanalyze it," he grunts.

That's the problem though. All through breakfast, I can't help but overanalyze this whole situation. A million questions run through my mind. The main one being: why is he being so nice to me?

I eat as much as I can stomach. Which isn't a lot. When I can't possibly eat another bite, I lay my knife and fork on the plate. Romeo scowls at all the food I didn't eat and I feel awful.

"I'm sorry. It's not your cooking. I promise. I just can't..." I let my sentence drift off.

"It's fine," he says, but I can tell he's bothered.

I look across the table to where Sandra and Luca are sharing weird looks with each other, like they're both in on a secret I'm not privy to.

When the doorbell rings, Romeo stands. "That will be the doc. Come on," he says to me. I don't think it was a request to follow him; it was more of an order. I should refuse to go blindly. But I want to get whatever this is over with, so I can just go home. Romeo leads me into the living room, returning moments later with an older man.

"How are you feeling?" the man asks.

"I'm good," I answer.

"No, she's not. She was throwing up and has barely eaten anything this morning," Romeo speaks over me.

"Okay. Ma'am, I'm just going to check your vitals. Is that okay with you?" The doctor turns to me.

"It's Livvy, and yes. But, really, I'm good," I insist.

"How's your head feeling?" the doctor asks. "After a dose of Rohypnol, it's normal to have a bit of a headache."

A bit? That's an understatement. I don't tell him this though. "It's okay. Not that bad."

He listens to my heart, checks my pulse, and takes my blood pressure before packing everything back into his bag. "You're very lucky. Last night could have ended very differently for you. But your vitals are good. I suggest plenty of water, and to take it easy for the rest of today," he says to me, then turns to Romeo with a firmer tone. "She's fine."

"Thanks for coming back, Doc," Romeo says. The doctor nods and leaves the room.

"I'm really sorry for all this. I'm going to go home and get out of your hair." I stand.

"You're not in my hair, Livvy. I'll drive you back to your dorm," Romeo says. "Wait here. I'll go grab my keys."

"You don't have to drive me. I can walk. Or get an Uber."

Romeo stalks out of the room, shaking his head no. I really do need to leave, get home, and clear my thoughts. Everything about this man confuses me.

Chapter Seven

Romeo

I dropped Livvy and Sandra back at their dorm building, giving the latter strict instructions not to leave the former's side today. And to keep me updated if anything happens.

"You know, if you weren't my brother, I'd shoot you to put you out of your misery right now," Luca says from the passenger seat of my car.

"What?"

"You. You're really hung up on this girl. It's not like you," he says.

"I'm not hung up on anyone," I deny.

"If you're not hung up on her, then you'll come out tonight, pick up some random piece of ass, and get the fuck over whatever hold Little Miss Sunshine has on you."

I glare at him. I know he's trying to goad me into a reaction, which is why I don't respond to that. "You can always jump out, you know. You don't have to come with me," I tell him.

"Yeah, okay. Like I'm going to miss all the fun." Luca smirks. We're on the way to the warehouse to pay a visit to the fucker who drugged Livvy. Luca found and kept him on ice for me. "I'm keen to see how you're going to explain all this to Pops, though?"

"He'll understand. He wouldn't stand for any girl being drugged, Luc. You know that."

"Maybe, but how interested is he going to be to learn that you've suddenly grown a heart and it's full of rainbow and sunshine. Mom will be planning your nuptials quicker than you can blink."

"Fuck off. She's my tutor. That's all."

"Does she know that?" I don't answer, but he keeps talking anyway. "Right, well, when you're done lying to yourself, let me know so I can say *I told you so*." He laughs.

"Whatever." I pull into the parking lot and groan.

"What the fuck are those two doing here?" I ask, glaring at our older brothers, Theo and Matteo.

"Ruining any chance of fun we had. Like always." Luca rolls his eyes.

I turn the engine off and jump out of the car. Matteo is aiming his shit-eating, smart-ass grin at me, while Theo is sending us his usual pissed-off glare. You'd think I just ran over his cat or something. "You know, when I was told *my delivery* was in the warehouse, I was curious because I didn't place any Amazon orders. Imagine my surprise when I called Pops and found out he hadn't been shopping either. So we dialed Matteo, and nope, the request didn't come from him. Which leaves you two morons. Care to tell me what the fuck you ordered?" Theo asks.

"Does it really matter if I'm spending my own money?" I counter.

"It does, when your funds are attached to my bank accounts."

Okay, all this riddle talk is starting to piss me off. "The fucker in there date-rape drugged a friend." I lift one shoulder up.

"What friend? You don't have any friends?" Matteo presses.

"Fuck off. I have plenty of friends, asshole. Now, if you two don't mind, I have shit to do."

"By all means, don't let me stop you from opening your package." Theo holds an arm out towards the door to the warehouse.

Rolling my eyes at his dramatics, I walk past both him and Matteo and enter the building, heading straight for the back room where I know this asshole will be tied up. And, sure enough, when I enter, the fucker is hanging from metal chains, piss stains spotting his jeans. From the looks of it, the retrieval company already did a number on him.

"Do you know who I am?" I ask, stepping right up to him.

"Should I?" he asks back.

"You should always know the name of the man who's going to kill you," I tell him. "Romeo Valentino." I watch as recognition and fear cross his face in equal measure.

"I don't know anything. I didn't do anything," he says.

"Really, you don't remember being in a club last night? I guess you also don't remember slipping drugs into a girl's water bottle?"

He violently shakes his head no.

"Because I sure as fuck remember you sitting right next to her. Strawberry blonde, tight little black dress, bright-blue eyes? Ring a bell?"

"She needed to loosen up a bit, man. Girl was frigid as fucking ice."

My fist connects with his mouth, and his lip splits open on impact.

"Ah, fuck," he yells.

"That's just the beginning. That girl happens to be

57

a good friend of mine. And you know what happens to people who try to fuck over friends of mine?"

"No."

"I'd tell you to go and ask them, but no one in that position has been able to talk again." Bending down, I retrieve the knife from my boot. "You know, I've always been fascinated with how quickly a body can drain of blood when you slice the veins in the ankle." I turn towards my three brothers, who are all standing there with curious gazes locked on me. "You want to take a wager on how long it will take?" I ask them.

"Ten grand, I say five minutes." Theo is the first to speak up.

"I'll match your ten and say seven," Luca counters.

"Four minutes," Matteo adds.

"Considering he's usually the one with the knife..." I gesture to Matteo. "I'm going with his bet," I say to the nameless asshole. "Let's find out, shall we?" I smirk at him.

"What? No, stop. I'm sorry! I didn't know. It won't happen again. I swear."

"No, it won't fucking happen again," I tell him as I reach for his left leg. He kicks and thrashes it around, trying to escape the blade.

He can fight all he wants, because nothing is going to stop me. All I can think about when I bring the knife's edge to his ankle, cutting right into the vein, is a passed-out, helpless Livvy and what would have happened to her if I wasn't there. He screams in agony.

Dropping his leg, I move onto the other one, repeating the process. I then push to my feet and walk over to the button on the wall that operates the pulley system he's presently chained to. The metal clinks as I press the button and his body is lifted higher in the air. His feet hang loosely as red liquid drains from the open wounds. I step back and watch the minutes tick by on my watch. When the flow stops and his body hangs lifeless in the air, no longer swinging with his piss-poor efforts to save himself, I turn around and smile at my brothers.

"Matteo was bang on. Pay up," I tell them. It doesn't surprise me in the least that Matteo was right. People might fear Theo the most out of all of us. But Matteo is by far the most ruthless, merciless made man I've ever met. I'm just glad the asshole's my brother and not my foe.

"So this was all over a girl?" Theo asks, without any readable expression on his face.

"No, this was about getting rid of one more sick fuck in the world," I tell him.

"Right. Well, I've got shit to do. Make sure you two clean this shit up." Theo walks out.

"Nice chat, bro!" I yell out to his retreating form. To which, he simply sticks a hand up in the air and flips me the bird.

* * *

I've just showered and flopped myself on my bed with my laptop. I might not need tutoring or to study at all really, but I do still have essays due. Unlike Luca, I don't have grand plans of being a professional NFL player. I actually don't even know what my plans are after college. I'm guessing I'll just help out with the family businesses. Logging into my emails, I see one from Livvy. The subject line reads: *I'm sorry this is late.* I click it open.

Dear Romeo,

I hope you accept my deepest apologies for the events of last night and this morning. If you want me to recommend other tutors for you, I completely understand. However, in the meantime, I've put together some study notes for you to review.

Again, thank you for everything you did to help me.

Kindest Regards,
Livvy

. . .

There's an attachment to the email. It's three pages of study notes on the works of Jane Austen. Hitting reply, I try to calm the rising irritation before I type. She shouldn't even be thinking about studying today. The doctor told her to rest and here she is, compiling study notes for other people. And I feel like fucking shit, because I don't even need the damn notes.

Subject: You're supposed to be resting.

Dear Livvy,

I have no intention of ever requiring another tutor. Why would I swap when I already have the best? I appreciate the study notes, but you're on doctor's orders to rest. Why aren't you resting?

Yours,
   Romeo

. . .

Her reply comes immediately.

Subject: I'm well rested...

Dear Romeo,

Thank you for your concern. But I am well rested. Studying helps me relax. Weird, I know, but it is what it is.

Livvy

I can't stop the grin on my face.

Subject: Not weird.

Dear Livvy,

If the world were filled with more people like you, humankind would be better off. If

studying helps you relax, I'm free to be your study buddy any day.

Yours,
   Romeo

I wait ten minutes, my eyes glued to the screen. She doesn't reply. Fuck, did I come on too strong? I'm way out of my element with this girl. I also don't know if I want to, or am ready, to follow up on this unbreakable pull I have towards her. Matteo's been best friends with a girl his whole life—granted, he's also been in love with her his whole life. But their weird relation-ship works for them.

Maybe Livvy is my first actual friend other than Luca?

Chapter Eight

Livvy

I'm nervous. Again.

I should have told him I can't tutor him. The problem is that I actually like talking to him. I like being around him, which is weird because I don't usually like being around a lot of people. Hopefully, I can get past this crush I have and tutor him. I just have to remind myself that, that's the reason he's here. For me to help him pass English Lit, not anything else.

Which is ridiculous. Why would he be here for any other reason? I pull my hair out of the straight ponytail I spent half an hour perfecting this morning and pile it up in my usual messy bun on top of my head. I need to bring myself back down to earth. Besides, even if he were here because I woke up in an alternate universe where girls like me got the attention of boys like Romeo, I shouldn't be trying to be someone I'm not. I've never bothered to try to please men before, and I'm not going to start now. Except, when I see him approaching the table, see that wicked smile directed right at me, those damn butterflies start dancing in my stomach. And I find myself sitting up straighter.

"Hey, how are you feeling?" Romeo asks, sitting in the chair right next to me, his eyes travelling around my face and searching for God only knows what.

"Better, thank you." My hands busy themselves straightening my notebook and pens in front of me that were already straight.

"This is for you." Romeo hands me a paper coffee cup from the café that's outside the library.

"Thank you." I take the offered cup, noticing he doesn't have one. "Did you not get yourself one?" I ask him, confused. Why would he stop and get me a coffee if he wasn't getting himself one too?

"I don't drink coffee," he says.

"Oh." Yep, that's about the level of my intelligence right now. I'm reduced to one-word answers.

"I looked over the notes you sent. They were great,

although you shouldn't have been working when you were supposed to be resting."

"I find studying, learning, relaxing. I know it's odd but reading is how I rest," I answer, opening my notebook.

"It's not odd. It's... endearing," he says.

"Well, I can see why you're in English Lit." I smile.

"Oh, yeah, why's that?" he asks.

"Because you're really good with words." I can feel the blush rising up my chest and I have to look away. Opening my notebook, I look at the list of topics I thought would be helpful to go over in today's session. "What did you think of the passage I sent you from *Pride and Prejudice*?"

"That Mr. Darcy is a complete ass," he says.

"What? Why?" I can't keep the shock out of my voice. "I happen to be a huge fan of Mr. Darcy," I defend.

"Tell me why you believe that Darcy and Elizabeth were compatible. They came from different worlds. Her mother would have been happy to sell her to the highest bidder. If anything, *Pride and Prejudice* is woman's way of representing Darwinism at its finest."

He cannot be serious? But as I look into his eyes, I can tell he is deadly so.

"Next, you'll tell me you love the whole *Romeo and Juliet* nonsense too," he adds before I can even come up with a response to his first ridiculous statement.

"Actually, I do. It's the most beautiful love story of

all time," I say proudly. "And women marrying is not a way of survival. It's a way of life, especially in the era of Austen." I feel like we are talking in circles. We've already had this conversation.

"But they didn't have to marry rich men. They could have lived out their duties of being baby makers to a poor man just as well. They chose rich, because they wanted the best chance at survival in a harsh world. Darwinism," he says, as if it's that simple. "And *Romeo and Juliet* is anything but beautiful. Everyone and anyone knows you don't sleep with the enemy. They both paid for that mistake with their lives and took the lives of their supposed loved ones with them."

"I don't know about that. Their love was so strong that neither of them could imagine a life without the other in it. It was bittersweet." I'm not even sure why I feel the need to defend the love story, but I do.

"It was codependency, not love. Love isn't meant to end in death."

I tilt my head and look at him, really look at him. I may have Googled him last night—curiosity got the better of me. Let's just say what I read about him, about his family, well, it should have been enough to have me cancelling these tutoring sessions. "Are you saying you wouldn't kill for the person you love?"

Romeo shrugs. "What angle do you think I should use with this essay?"

I guess that's a *no* then. I'm a little thankful he changed the subject. Because, frankly, after reading up about him being a suspected mafia prince, I don't think I want the answer to that question. Even though it's hypothetical, I shouldn't have asked it.

"Well, since you're so against the concept of love, you should focus on the time period and the expectations of women."

"I'm not against love." He frowns.

"Okay?" I'm not really sure where to go with this. I don't want to get into this topic with him. It's making me nervous. I don't like it. Instead, I open a few books and start guiding him on what to look for in the passages. Eventually, I've talked about as much as I can on the subject matter. Closing the books and piling them up on the table, I pack my own things away before standing. "Here, take this and check it out. Read through it, and next time we meet, we can start writing up notes for your paper." I hand him a copy of *Pride and Prejudice*.

"I've read it. I know the story," he says, pushing to his feet. He doesn't take the book.

I look down at my watch. We've spent longer here than I intended. I'm dreading the walk back to my dorm alone. I would ask Sandra to meet me but I know she's having dinner with her parents tonight.

"What's wrong?" Romeo asks.

"Ah, nothing. I didn't realize how late it was." I try to keep the fear out of my voice. I can see by the concern on his face that I failed.

"Did you drive here?" he asks me.

"My dorm is a five-minute walk. Also, it's New York. People don't drive."

"I've lived in the city my whole life and I drive." He picks up his backpack and then takes mine out of my hands. "Come on, I'll walk you to your dorm."

"Oh, you don't have to do that." My protest is weak. Because, honestly, I'm relieved he offered.

"Yes, I do. My mother would have my balls if she found out I let a girl walk home alone at night." Romeo holds his arm out in the direction of the stairs. "After you."

"Thank you," I say, walking past him.

We're both quiet as we exit the library. I can't help but look around once we're outside. I wish I could shake this feeling, the one that I'm being watched. It's only ever when I'm leaving the library at night. It's probably my dad's horror stories finally kicking in and making me paranoid. I mean, who would be watching *me*?

"What are you looking for?" Romeo asks, staring at my face.

"Nothing," I lie and stare straight ahead.

"Right," he says, pulling his phone from his pocket and typing out a message to someone. When we get to my dorm building, he hands me my bag.

"Thank you," I say, looking past him. I swear I just saw someone on the other side of the road. But it's a campus. There's bound to be people around.

Romeo turns his head and looks in the direction

that I was staring. "Is someone bothering you, Livvy?" he asks.

"What? No. I just... it's stupid." I shake my head.

"You're not capable of stupid. What is it?" he presses.

"I've just had this feeling like I'm being watched when I walk back at night. That's all. Like I said, it's stupid."

"It's not stupid." He glares up and down the path. There's nobody in sight though.

"Want me to stick around for a bit?" he asks.

"No, I'm fine. Thank you for walking me home. I'll see you on Tuesday."

"Sure, thanks again for all your help. I really do appreciate it."

"Anytime." I smile and force myself to turn around and walk into the building.

Why is it always so hard to walk away from him? He has some kind of magnetic pull on me, an invisible force tying me to him.

Chapter Nine

Romeo

Walking back to the library, I answer the slew of text messages that have been blowing up my phone for the last few hours. Most of them from Luca. I don't think I ever noticed how fucking needy he was before. I guess because I've always been available to him. Now, my mind is preoccupied with everything that is Livvy.

Which is fucked up, because Luca has always been my number one. He still is. At least I think he is.

The drive back to my apartment is short. I open the door and find Luca and a bunch of his football buddies drinking out on the balcony. "Finally, where the fuck have you been?" he asks the moment I walk in.

"Out," I answer.

"Well, get a drink. We're celebrating." He smiles.

"Oh, yeah? What's the occasion?"

"It's Monday."

"You're celebrating because it's Monday?" I ask. Surely I didn't hear that right.

"Every day we're still breathing is worth celebrating, bro." He smirks.

Ain't that the fucking truth.

In our family, it's a fucking gift, each day we wake up breathing. That thought brings me back to Livvy's question. Would I kill for love? *I've killed for less,* I wanted to tell her. I wanted to open my mouth and spill all of my darkest secrets. Shit, that could see me behind bars for the rest of my life. She's fucking dangerous. I need to put distance between myself and her. If only I could fucking resist her orbit... I can't fucking help but want to be close to her. And I haven't even so much as kissed the girl. Yet.

"I've got to study," I lie, pivoting on my heel and heading in the opposite direction. I don't feel like drinking with Luca's friends. I don't feel like pretending. Instead, I close myself inside the sanctuary of my room. My mind replays the image of Livvy sprawled out on my bed. I can't wait to get her back in here. Only conscious this time. And naked.

Sitting on my bed, I open my laptop, click my video messenger app, and call my cousin Izzy. She's always understood me the best out of anyone. My brothers get me. I could always go to them for advice. The only problem with asking them anything about Livvy is they're all horrible gossips and it'd just get back to my mom. Nobody, especially me, needs my mother getting it in her head that I'm about to give her a daughter-in-law. She's obsessed with marrying all of us boys off. She wants enough grandbabies to fill her house. And the house I grew up in is fucking huge. Fifteen bedrooms to be exact. That's a lot of fucking grandbabies—ones I have no intention of giving her.

Izzy's face comes into view. "Romeo, Romeo, what can I do for you?" she asks with a devilish twinkle in her eyes. She knows how much I hate any reference to Shakespeare, which is precisely why she makes every effort to address me using her best rendition of Juliet.

I roll my eyes. "Izzy, can't I just call my cousin to say hi?"

"You could, but you don't. So spit it out. Unlike you, I'm not living the college life. I actually have shit to do."

"I do shit," I defend.

"Yep, sure you do."

"There's this girl," I start.

"Wait. Stop right there," she yells, jumping up. I watch as she runs to a window to peer outside.

"What's wrong? Izzy, what the fuck is going on?" I'm ready to make the one-hour trip to her house.

She finally sits back down in front of the computer. "Sorry, had to check if there were any flying pigs outside because I thought you just said you had a girl."

"Funny, maybe I should call another cousin. I'm sure Lily and Hope wouldn't give me as much grief."

"Meh, you know they'd be worse."

I hate that she's right. My other cousins, Lily and Hope, would go straight to their mom, my Aunt Reilly, who would then go straight to my mother with this gossip.

"Okay, stop pouting. It's ruining your good looks. Now, tell me about this girl and what the problem is," Izzy says, her expression more serious.

"The problem is she makes me feel... different."

"Different? How so?"

"I don't know, Iz. I've never had these feelings before, for anyone. It's like when I'm not with her, all I can think about is finding ways to be with her. When I am with her, I never want to leave."

"Romeo, you're besotted with the girl. In love." She smiles.

"I'm not in love," I deny.

"Does this girl have a name? Where'd you meet her?"

"Livvy. I met her in the library."

"The library? As in the building filled with dust and books?" Her face screws up in disgust.

"Yes, that one."

"What were you doing in the library?" Izzy asks.

"I'm a college student. We study, Iz."

"You don't study, Romeo."

"I do, since I discovered how hot chicks in the library are."

"So... she's hot?"

"Insanely beautiful," I tell her.

"Has Luca met this mystery woman?"

"Yes."

"And what does he think?"

"He thinks I've lost my mind. Which isn't far from the truth. I can't fucking function. I almost told her tonight, you know. Who I really am, things I've done."

"That's probably not a good idea. Some things are best never said aloud, Romeo."

"I know that."

"Does she feel the same way about you?"

"I don't know. How the fuck am I supposed to know that?"

Izzy blinks at me with shock on her face. "You're putting the Valentino name to shame, Romeo. No Valentino man has ever had an issue picking up chicks."

"I don't have an issue. She's not just a chick, Iz, and I'm not trying to pick her up."

"You really like her. Does she know you like her?

Have you actually even spoken to her yet? Or are we still in the stalking stage of the relationship?"

"I haven't stalked her."

Izzy raises her brows at me in question.

"Much. I may have listened to a few of her conversations with other students she tutors. But that's not stalking."

"Actually, it is, Romeo. Anyway, why don't you just ask her out if you like her? Take her on a date."

"A date? Doing what?"

"Oh my god, you cannot be this dense. Romeo, your namesake is shaking in his grave right now."

Again, I roll my eyes at her.

"Fine... dinner, movie, dancing. What does she like?"

"She likes books. She's smart, extremely smart."

"So you have that in common then."

"Except she thinks I need tutoring."

Izzy's laughter comes bellowing out of the speakers. "Excuse me? What? Why on earth would she think that?"

"Because I told her I did."

"Oh my god, this is better than *Jerry Springer* reruns."

"I'm glad my life amuses you," I groan.

"Okay, I'm sorry. You're either going to have to tell her you like her and take the plunge, or wait around and watch as another guy discovers how great she is and steals her from underneath your friend-zoned nose."

"I'm not in the friend zone," I deny. At least I fucking hope I'm not.

"Yet."

My phone vibrates next to me. I pick it up, seeing Sandra's name on my screen. She never calls me. Why the fuck would she be calling me now?

"Iz, I gotta go." Slamming my laptop closed, I click answer and bring my phone to my ear. "Sandra, what's wrong?" I ask her.

"Who have you pissed off, Romeo?" she hisses through the receiver.

"Too many people to list. You'll need to be more specific."

"Someone is targeting Livvy, and the only reason I can possibly think for someone to do that is *you*."

I freeze, my muscles tense, and my heart rate increases. "What the fuck did you say?"

"Someone has put a target on Livvy's back. She doesn't have enemies, Romeo. People like her. I knew I should have kept her away from you. Even after she Googled you herself last night, she was still insistent on tutoring you."

"What do you mean someone put a target on her? Where the fuck is she, Sandra?" I yell, stand up, slide my feet back into my boots, and grab my keys.

"Someone broke into our dorm room and spray-painted the word *slut* across her bed. And all over the walls on her side of the room."

"Why the fuck would someone do that?"

"That's what I was hoping you could tell me?"

"I'm coming now. Stay there."

"No, you need to stay away from her, Romeo. She's too good for the likes of your world. She doesn't deserve this."

Hanging up on Sandra, because fuck her and anyone else if they think I'm going to stay away from Livvy, I run into Luca in the hallway. "What's going on?" he asks.

"Someone broke into Livvy's dorm."

"Why? What'd they take?"

"I don't think they took anything. They spray-painted *slut* across her bed and walls."

"Sure that wasn't meant for Sandra?" Luca smirks.

"Sandra seems certain it was purposely done on Livvy's side of the room."

"Why would anyone target her?" Luca asks.

I raise an eyebrow at him. It's not a fucking coincidence that the moment I start showing interest in her, someone is fucking targeting her. This is why people in our world shouldn't mix with people like Livvy. Sandra's right. She doesn't fucking deserve it. And whoever did this to her will fucking find that out the hard way.

"Okay, just give me a sec. I'm coming with you."

Luca jogs back out to the deck, says something to his friends, and jogs back to the front door.

I make it to Livvy's dorm building in half the time it should take to drive there. Pulling up out front, I jump out of the car and run up the steps. The door's fucking locked. Luca is right behind me. He leans over and enters a code into the keypad.

"How do you know the code?" I ask him.

"It's a girls' dorm? Bro, do you really think I don't know the code?"

Ignoring him, I rush up the three flights of stairs, too impatient to wait for the elevator. When I get to her door, it's already open, and there are four girls in the room. None of whom are Livvy. "Where is she?" I ask Sandra.

She points to their bathroom.

"Why the fuck are you all in here?" I turn to the other girls standing around Sandra. None of them answer me, just look at me with their mouths hanging open. "Get the fuck out," I tell them.

When no one starts moving, I look to Luca.

"Now!" he yells more firmly. That's when they scamper out. Luca shuts the door behind them and then pulls a scanning device out of his back pocket. Flicking it on, his finger goes to his lips as he walks around the room holding the device up in various positions. He's searching for microphones or hidden cameras. I don't know why anyone would want to plant a device in Livvy's dorm room. Sandra, maybe. Her father is an associate of the family. But Livvy, no one should even fucking know about her existence yet.

I knock on the bathroom door. "Livvy, open the door."

I hear shuffling before it opens a crack. Livvy's eyes are red and puffy. Shit, she's been fucking crying. I push the door in, forcing her to take a step backwards to allow me room to enter, shut it behind me, and look at her. I want to fucking kill the bastard who brought these tears to her eyes. My hands shake with the need for retribution.

"What are you doing here?" Livvy asks when I don't say anything.

"I... Sandra called and told me someone broke in. What happened?"

"I don't know. It's probably just some stupid prank," she says. "Right?"

"Probably... I'll get this place cleaned up for you, but you're not staying here tonight. Pack a bag." My hand reaches for the door.

"Wait, I have to stay here. I don't have anywhere else to go, Romeo."

My eyebrows draw down at her. Is she fucking serious right now? "You're staying at my place. Come on."

"I... I can't stay at your place. I'll be fine here. It's not that bad."

"It was bad enough to make you fucking cry, Livvy. You're coming to sleep at my place tonight. Tomorrow

I'll have new locks put on your door and that shit will be cleaned up."

"Why? I mean, I don't want to sound ungrateful because I'm not, but why are you doing this? Why are you here, Romeo? Why are you being so nice to me?"

"Because you're my friend, and I'm not the kind of guy who lets their friends get fucked with," I tell her, cursing *myself* for putting *myself* in the fucking friend zone.

"Okay." She smiles. "I don't think I've ever had a friend as nice as you, though. Well, apart from Sandra."

"That's... sad."

She laughs. "Shockingly, I wasn't all that popular in high school. Then I came here and met Sandra." She lifts one shoulder up and down.

"High school popularity is overrated, trust me. Come on, let's get out of here."

"I just need to finish washing this paint off my hands." Livvy holds her palms up. They're covered in the red paint from her room. She must've been trying to scrub the walls by hand.

"Soap isn't going to scrub that off. I've got some stuff at the apartment that will remove it better."

"Are you sure? You don't have to do this. I can stay here, really. I'll be fine."

I open the door, holding it ajar for her. "Pack a bag, unless you want to borrow more of my clothes." I smirk, my eyes flicking up and down as I remember how she looked in my sweatshirt.

"I'll pack some things." She averts her gaze.

There's a knock at the door while we're waiting for Livvy to pack the clothes. Luca curses, glancing down at his device. "Did you call the cops?" he asks Sandra, disdain evident in his voice.

"What? No. I called *him*." Sandra points to me.

"Livvy, did you?" Luca questions.

I don't know why, but my instincts to protect her against anyone take over, and I step in front of her. Blocking Luca's view. He lifts one brow at me, silently asking me if I'm serious right now.

You bet your ass I'm serious.

Livvy steps around me, her arms folded at her waist. "No, I can't have a report about this. Oh god, if my dad finds out, he's going to be here by morning."

"Why would your dad find out?" Luca asks, curious.

"He's a retired police officer. He has friends in New York, who like to keep him updated on everything and anything to do with this college," Livvy says.

Luca points a finger at Livvy. "You're dad's a cop?" His finger then moves to me. "And you're... you." He shakes his head from side to side. "Fottuto idiota, Romeo. Mi stai prendendo in giro adesso?" *Fucking idiot, Romeo. Are you kidding me now?* Luca fires off in rapid Italian.

"Stai zitto." *Shut up*, I growl back at him.

"Di tutte le fottute ragazze, dovevi scegliere la figlia di un poliziotto di cui innamorarti." *Of all the fucking girls, you had to pick a cop's daughter to fall in love with.*

I'm about to fucking hit the motherfucker to get him to shut up.

"Aspetta cosa intendi?" *What do you mean?* Both of our heads spin to Livvy, who just replied to us in perfect Italian.

"Conosci l'italiano?" *You know Italian?* I ask her.

"I know many languages. What is he talking about, Romeo?" she asks me.

"Nothing. Forget it. He's an idiot." I walk to the door and open it, since the knocking isn't stopping. "Can I help you?"

"Yeah, there was a report of vandalism?" Campus security is standing in the hall.

Chapter Ten

Livy

I feel awkward. I should have insisted on staying in my dorm room. The problem is I have a really hard time saying no to Romeo. Which is a dangerous position to be in. After he talked the campus security into not lodging the complaint, which surprisingly wasn't that hard for him to do, we went to his apartment.

He escorted me to his room, took me into his bathroom, and washed the paint off my hands with some kind of liquid soap he had in a clear unlabeled bottle. He then walked out and told me he'd be downstairs. I showered and changed into a pair of yoga pants and a baggy shirt. Now I'm debating whether to just jump out the window, which I'm not even sure if it opens or not. Probably not, considering we're so high up. Or my other option is to go downstairs and try not to be as awkward as I'm feeling.

Inhaling a deep breath, I choose door number two —well, the only door. However, the closer I get, the more I hear Luca's words. *You chose a cop's daughter to fall in love with.* Neither Romeo nor I brought up that can of worms. Luca has to be wrong. There is no way Romeo Valentino is in love with me. He doesn't even know me. And if he did, he certainly wouldn't be in love with me. He's the kind of man who will end up married to some stunning supermodel, not the girl next door. There is a little part of me that wonders what life with Romeo as a boyfriend, lover, would be like. If he's this attentive as a friend, then whoever he ends up with will be one lucky girl. I don't allow myself to dream of that girl ever being me. I may be a hopeless romantic, but I refuse to live my life with my head in the clouds. This is reality, not a fictional love story for the ages.

As soon as I enter the living room, Romeo and Luca stop whatever heated conversation they were having. "You okay?" Romeo asks, walking over to me.

"Uh-huh." I look between the two brothers. I could

cut the tension with a knife. "I'm really sorry if I'm imposing... I can go..."

"You're not imposing," Romeo grunts and glares at Luca.

"No, you're not. Come on, come eat. I didn't know what you liked so I ordered a bit of everything," Luca says, pointing to the Chinese takeout containers that are scattered across the coffee table.

"I'll eat anything. I'm not picky," I tell him, taking a seat on the sofa.

"Obviously, if you're friends with this one, your standards are low." Luca laughs, gesturing a thumb at his twin as he plops down on a single chair opposite me. Romeo sits next to me on the sofa.

"I don't know. I happen to think he's a great choice for a friend," I defend Romeo.

"You two are something else." Luca laughs again. Romeo is silent as he loads up a plate with a bit of everything from each of the ten containers. He then hands it to me.

"You don't actually expect me to be able to eat all of this, do you?" I ask him.

"Not all of it," he grunts.

"Maybe you could add conversational skills to those tutoring sessions of yours, Liv," Luca comments.

"There's nothing wrong with his language skills," I deadpan.

"You know I'm joking, right? I'm his twin. Trust

me when I say there is no one in this world who has his back more than I do."

"Sorry, I didn't mean..." I don't even know what I'm apologizing for.

"It's fine. Ignore him, Livvy. Ma dropped him on his head when he was a baby," Romeo says.

"That would explain a lot," I murmur.

"Funny, you two should really go into the comedy business. All that intellect between the both of you is wasted."

"What are your plans for after college?" I ask Luca, trying to move us on to nicer, more normal conversation.

"Pro football. What about you?" he asks.

"Prosecuting attorney," I say proudly. Luca chokes on his food and I feel Romeo's body stiffen next to me. "What?" I ask them both.

"You... seriously? I can't... Well, Romeo, it was nice knowing ya. Let me know when Pops hears about this one. I don't want to miss your last words, bro." Luca stands and walks out of the room, shaking his head as he goes.

"What is he talking about?" I turn to Romeo.

"Nothing. Like I said, ignore almost everything that comes out of his mouth."

"So, it's not because your dad is a mob boss and you two are the princes of the Valentino family?"

"Where did you hear that?" Romeo smirks.

"Google."

"Don't believe everything you read on the internet, Livvy. You're smarter than that."

"So you're not a mafia prince?"

Romeo stares at me, searching my face. After what seems like an eternity, he sighs. "I don't want to lie to you. I can't. So, I'm asking you, begging you, don't ask me questions you're not ready to hear the answers to. Please." He's serious.

"I'm sorry. I didn't mean to make you feel like you have to tell me anything. You really don't need to. It's fine."

"That's the problem. I know I don't have to tell you shit but I want to. And I fucking can't," he says, looking away.

"Want to play a game?" I attempt to change the subject.

"What kind of game?"

"Twenty questions. If we're going to be friends, there're some things we should know about each other."

His smile drops. "Liv, I can't." He shakes his head.

"No, not like that, normal questions. Like what's your favorite color?"

"Blue," he says, staring into my eyes.

"Okay, it's your turn. Ask me a question."

"What's your favorite flower?"

"Mmm, lily of the valley," I tell him.

"Huh, I would have picked sunflowers. But those

little Mary's tears flowers are much more you. Delicate, sweet, beautiful."

I can feel the redness creeping up my chest and neck. "Okay, my turn. Favorite television show?"

"Easy, *The Sopranos*," he deadpans.

"Really? Why?"

"That's another question. It's my turn. Why'd you come to college in New York?" he asks.

I think about the answer. "I grew up in a very small town. Everyone knows everyone. It was nice—don't get me wrong. I love going home for small periods of time. I chose New York because of the people. Nobody knows me here. I can be anyone. I can do anything I want and no one will know." I lift a shoulder. "It's stupid, but my safe little southern town was suffocating. I was drowning under the weight of everyone's expectations. Fearing that I'd end up a southern belle wife. Married to a man I didn't love."

"You don't want the white picket fence, 2.5 kids?" Romeo asks.

"That's another question. But, no, I don't want that. Well, I do. Kind of. I want a love that never dies, fire, passion. I want the kind of love Romeo and Juliet had. Just, you know, without the death part. I want adventure. I want a career. I want it all and I don't want to have to choose one or the other."

"You shouldn't ever have to choose or settle for anything less than that."

"Thank you. My turn. First kiss?" I ask.

"That's not a question," he says.

"How old were you when you had your first kiss?"

"Twelve."

"Twelve? Really? Like a real kiss? With a girl? Or *a boy*, I don't judge."

"Yes, twelve, and it was a girl." He laughs. "How about you?"

"Sixteen. On my sixteenth birthday, actually."

"What was his name?" Romeo asks a little too casually. It's an odd tone for him.

"Kirk, my high school boyfriend." I smile.

"What happened to Kirk?"

"He dumped me the day I told him I was coming to New York."

"He's a fucking assclown," Romeo grunts.

"No, he's not. He just wanted a different life from what I wanted."

"Are you still in love with him?"

"No, I'm not really sure I was ever in love with him. We were friends before we were anything else. It was easy. Comfortable," I say. "What about you? Ever had your heart broken? A girl who got away?"

"No, you'd have to have a heart for it to be broken. I don't think I've ever liked anyone enough for that."

"Huh, interesting."

"What's interesting?" he asks.

"You think you don't have a heart, but you do. I've seen it," I tell him.

"We've already established that when it comes to

90

matters of the heart, your perception is wrong, Livvy. Do we really need to revisit the *Romeo and Juliet* debate?"

I can't help the smile that spreads across my face. I actually feel like I could debate any topic with him and still have a good time. "I don't want to hurt your ego when I prove you wrong." I laugh.

Chapter Eleven

Romeo

Hearing Livvy's carefree laugh eases my tensed muscles. I feel like I've been walking on pins and needles, waiting for the other shoe to drop. I know that we can never actually go anywhere. She wants to be a fucking prosecutor. And me, well, I'm the one she'll be prosecuting. Or one of my family members...

It couldn't be more of a fucked-up situation. If I

can't have her, the least I can do is keep a close eye on her. Keep her safe. Starting with finding out what fuckwit spray-painted her dorm room.

"If you won, it'd be because I let you," I tell her in response to her statement about beating me in a debate.

"If that's what you have to tell yourself to sleep at night. I was on the debate team. We won state champs three years in a row."

"Of course you were," I say, rolling my eyes. "Tell me a flaw. There has to be something you can't do?"

"Mmm, my biggest flaw is my inability to make friends. I've never really been able to just *hang out*," she says, using air quotes.

"You're doing it just fine now."

"That's because you are easy to talk to. Easy to be around. I don't know... It's weird but I feel like I've known you a lot longer than a week."

"It's not weird," I tell her and she raises one eyebrow at me. "Okay, it's a little weird, but I feel it too, you know. This connection."

"Oh."

An awkward silence washes over us. I've never been this fucking awkward, this scared of saying the wrong fucking thing before. "You can sleep in my bed. I'll stay here on the sofa."

"I'm not kicking you out of your bed, Romeo. I'll stay on the sofa. It's fine."

"I'm not having you sleep on the sofa." I stand. "Come on." Taking hold of her open palm, I pull her to her feet and walk down the hall. I don't let go. I know I should, but fuck, it feels good to hold her hand. "I won't sleep if you're on the sofa. Take the bed. I'll be fine. Trust me," I tell her, opening the door.

"I feel horrible, Romeo. You shouldn't lose your bed because of me," she says.

I'd offer to share it with her, but I don't want to make her uncomfortable. So, instead, I smile. "If I cared, I wouldn't offer it. Help yourself to anything you want, or yell out if you need me for anything." I stalk back down the hall.

"Romeo?"

I turn around to face her.

"Thank you," she says before closing my bedroom door.

I go into the kitchen and pour myself a tumbler of whiskey. Is Luca right? Am I in love with her? How the fuck am I supposed to know the answer to that? How does anyone really know if they're in love, or just lusting after the unattainable?

Heading back into the living room, I clear away all the takeout leftovers and wipe down the table before I crack my laptop open. I had one of the boys log in to the dorm security and get the footage from today. Their email says the system was cut off for an hour and no one was seen entering or leaving Livvy's floor. She told me she feels like she's being watched. Maybe she fucking is. I know the footage isn't there, but I look for myself anyway, fast-forwarding through most of the day. There's nothing that appears off about the girls who come and go from the building. Why didn't I fucking plant a camera or listening device in her dorm room? I had thought of it. But something about crossing a line and some other bullshit morals held me back from following through with that plan.

Well, those morals can fuck right off now, because I want cameras everywhere she fucking goes. I won't allow her to be a target, especially if it's someone trying to get at me. Shutting off the laptop, I lie flat on my back and close my eyes.

* * *

Downing a cup of black coffee, in my attempts to pick myself up a bit after a night spent tossing and turning, I slam the empty cup on the counter. I'm cooking breakfast, one of the only meals I can make that's also half decent. Luca is the first one to enter the kitchen. "Maybe Livvy should sleep here more often if this is what I get to wake up to."

I don't bother responding. I'm still pissed off at him for how much of a smart-ass he was to her last night.

"Silent treatment too. Perfect fucking morning," he continues.

I flip the pancakes, continuing to ignore his stupidity. Maybe if I pretend he isn't here, he'll go away.

"Really, Romeo, you're not gonna talk to me?"

"I don't have anything to say that you want to hear

right now, Luca."

"Good then, because I've got shit you need to hear. I get it. You like this chick. But her dad is a cop, Romeo. Just how do you think this is going to play out?"

"Former cop. Retired. He's not a cop anymore."

"And you think that makes a difference? That girl is way too fucking nice and innocent to get mixed up in our family, and you know it."

"You're right. She is. But what the fuck am I supposed to do, Luca? You know me better than anyone. I'm not going to be able to walk away from her."

"And if you don't walk away from her now, it's only going to get worse," he says.

"How about you try to not be a complete ass to her this morning. Don't make me hit you, Luca, because I won't hold back."

"You're not going to hit me, especially if she's in the same room as us. What would she think if she knew the real you, Romeo? Do you really think she'd still be here, sleeping next to you in your bed?"

"I slept on the sofa, asshole. And you know, I think she might be the only person who does know the real me." I see the hurt on his face. My words cut him deep. They're not true, but there is a side of me that I've only ever shown Livvy. A vulnerable side.

"Fuck you. If that's how you feel, then good luck to you. You might want to call Theo or Matteo, because when Pops finds out, you're gonna need a brother on your side and it won't fucking be me," he says, jumping to his feet like he's about to turn his back on me. Both literally and metaphorically.

"Sit the fuck back down. We both know it will always be you. Don't be so fucking dramatic," I tell him. It's always him and me against the world. Nothing is ever going to change that. Not even Livvy. I might be crazy about the girl, but Luca is and always will be my brother.

He throws himself on the chair with a groan. "I won't be doing it smiling," he grumbles.

"Good, because your smile is fucking ugly." I laugh.

"Where is Sleeping Beauty anyway?"

"Still asleep, I guess. I'm gonna go wake her up. Plate up this food for me, will ya."

"You know we could get a housekeeper to do this."

"Or you could pull the silver spoon out of your ass," I tell him, before exiting the kitchen.

Opening the bedroom door, I find Livvy still asleep on the bed. She looks so fucking peaceful, long strawberry blonde hair splayed out around her. I sit on the edge of the bed. My fingers brush her hair away from her face.

"Mmm," she mumbles something in her semi-conscious state.

"Livvy, it's time to wake up, babe." I lean down and whisper into her ear, inhaling her intoxicating scent of lavender and vanilla.

"Romeo?" she asks, slowly blinking her eyes open.

"Yeah?"

"Sleeping Beauty was woken up with a kiss, but I think waking up to your face might be even better."

I smile. She's still half-asleep and very much at ease. "Yeah, should we test the theory? Close your eyes," I whisper. She does as she's told. And, very slowly, I bring my lips down to her mouth. Just before they touch, I whisper, "Livvy, it's time to wake up, babe." Then I seal my lips on hers. Pressing ever so lightly. And I swear to fuck I have an out-of-body experience. I'm fucking floating. Some weird but good feeling runs through my veins. Pulling back, I open my eyes, connecting them with hers.

"I was wrong, the kiss was a much better way to wake up," she whispers.

"I'll keep that in mind next time I have to wake you up." I smile and push back off the bed. If I don't get out of this room now, I'm going to do something way better —or *worse*, depending how you look at it—than just peck her on the lips. "Come on, I've cooked you breakfast, and you have exactly one hour before your first class today."

"Shit, really?" She jumps out of bed. "How do you know when my classes are?"

"I looked it up," I tell her, taking hold of her palm and leading her to the kitchen. I don't miss the way Luca's eyes zone in on our joined hands.

Chapter Twelve

Livvy

Romeo dropped me off on campus out front of my first class. No, he didn't just drop me off. He parked the car, got out, and walked around to open my door. Then he handed me my bag, kissed my forehead, and said, "Separazione è un dolore così dolce." *Parting is such sweet sorrow.*

I finished the line, telling him, "I shall say goodnight till it be morrow."

He corrected me and said that he'd see me later today.

So, all day, I've been searching the crowds for him. Walking from one block to another with my head in the clouds. He kissed me. Romeo Valentino kissed me.

The question is *why*?

Was it simply because he was playing out the role of waking me up? Is that something a *friend* would do? Ugh, why is this so confusing? And why am I so hung up on him?

I haven't been able to focus on anything my professors have said today. I received a message from Sandra, asking me to meet her for a late lunch at the coffee shop near our building. That's where I'm headed now. I'm not looking forward to answering her million questions about Romeo. When I went to his place last night, Sandra went and stayed at her parents' penthouse. She extended the invite to me, saying I was welcome to come with her. In hindsight, I should have gone, but then I remember that kiss and wouldn't give that moment up for anything.

Walking into the coffee shop, I find Sandra seated in a booth. I smile as she looks up and waves me over. "Hey, sorry I'm late," I say, sitting opposite her.

"You're not late. I was early. I ordered for you." She points to the coffee, hamburger, and fries set out in front of me.

"Thank you. You're a lifesaver. I'm starving," I groan, popping a fry into my mouth.

"You're welcome. Now spill the deets. What the hell is going on with you and Romeo?"

"Nothing. We're friends," I tell her.

"Then why are you smiling like that—and blushing?"

"I'm just really happy to have this burger," I say, wrapping my mouth around the bun and taking a huge bite.

"Nice try. Really, Livvy, you need to be careful with those boys. The Valentinos aren't like other families," she whispers.

"I know. I Googled them too. But he's not like what the articles say. He's sweet and kind. And he is my friend."

"I've known those twins all my life, and no one has ever described either of them as *sweet* or *kind*."

"Well, maybe people have preconceived notions about who they are, instead of actually getting to know them." I lift one shoulder. "Have you been back to the dorm today?" I ask, changing the subject.

"Yep, lover boy had it repainted, Livvy. New bed linen is on your bed and a new lock on the door."

"How did he manage to do all that already?"

"He's a Valentino. He didn't do it himself. They have people for that."

"What do you mean *people*?"

"They have money, Livvy, the kind of money that can buy you whatever you want."

I choose to not question her about Romeo's family

100

anymore. If he wanted me to know something, he'd tell me. I'm sure.

An hour later, I'm running into the library for my Tuesday afternoon tutoring session.

I'm never late, and I'm not about to make today the first time for that. Sitting down at my usual table on the second floor, I open my notebooks. I'm meeting with Will, a business major who's struggling with his commerce class. Numbers are not my specialty. I prefer literature, but I can hold my own with the content. I've actually taught myself a lot by tutoring him.

William sits down in the seat opposite me. "Hey, how's your week been?" he asks.

"Good, busy. Yours?" I ask him. I've always had a good relationship with the students I tutor, but I don't make a habit of participating in chitchat. It eats into our allotted hour. Unless that student is Romeo. Somehow, being near him makes me forget I'm supposed to be helping him.

"Not bad. I was thinking... would you go out with me on Friday night?" he asks.

My eyes widen. Will has *never* indicated he was interested in dating me. "Ah, I can't. Sorry."

"Oh, if you're busy, we could go out Saturday instead?" he's quick to suggest.

"No, it's not that. I just... I'm sorry, Will, but I can't go out with you. I'm seeing someone," I lie.

"Oh, that's cool. No big deal." He tries to hide his

disappointment.

By the time the hour is up, I'm ready to never see him again. Which is ridiculous. He's been nothing but nice. There's just an awkwardness between us now.

"I'll see you next week," he says, walking away. I lean back into my seat and close my eyes momentarily. "Who is it that you're seeing?" Romeo's voice whispers into my ear, causing me to jump ten feet in the air.

"What the hell? Jesus, Romeo! You scared the hell out of me." My hand rests on my chest, my heart beating out of its cavity.

"Who is he? This guy you're seeing?" he asks again, sitting down next to me.

"What?" I ask, confused.

"You told Preppy that you were seeing someone? So, I want a name." His arms fold over his chest.

"I'm not seeing anyone, Romeo. I said that because I didn't want to hurt his feelings."

"Wrong answer, babe. Next time someone asks who you're seeing, be sure to tell them Romeo Valentino." He stands, leans over, and kisses my forehead. "Your next student is here," he says before stalking off.

My next student, Jonah, lowers himself into his chair, twisting his fingers together. "Hey, how are you?" I ask him with a smile, trying to shake off whatever that encounter was with Romeo.

"I, uh, I'm quitting tutoring. I'm really sorry, Liv. You've been great but I just... It's not working anymore, so I guess I'll see you around." He jumps up and leaves.

What the hell just happened? I don't like how he left like that. I thought we got along well. He was making progress, so why would he leave?

I open my email app and send him a message, asking if everything is okay. I really hope I didn't do anything to make him not want to work with me. I pack my books away. He was the last student I had to see this afternoon, and I don't feel like sitting around the library. Right now, I want to just stand under the spray of a steaming hot shower for at least thirty minutes and then curl up in my bed with a good book I can get lost in.

I walk out of the library door and am greeted by the wrong Valentino twin. "Luca, hey." I smile and wave awkwardly at him. I get the feeling he doesn't like me very much.

"How do you know I'm not Romeo?" he asks with a raised brow, seeming to realize it wasn't just a chance guess that first time at the restaurant.

"I just do. You're more... like a photocopy of him," I say with a shrug.

"A photocopy? I'm hurt." He holds a hand to his heart dramatically.

I smile. "No, you're not. What are you doing here?" I ask.

"Walking you home. You weren't supposed to finish for another hour though."

"Why are you walking me home?"

"Why'd you finish early?" he counters, taking my bag from my shoulder and swinging it over his.

"Jonah quit. Said he doesn't want me to tutor him anymore," I say.

"Why? What'd you do? Make him write lines?" he asks as he starts walking towards my dorm building.

"No. I honestly have no idea," I say, stepping next to him. We walk in silence for the rest of the way. It's not awkward, just comfortable. When we reach the entry to my dorm, I turn around and hold a hand out for my bag. "Thank you for escorting me home, but you really don't need to be doing this."

"Yes, I do. If my brother asks me to watch out for you, then I'm going to do it," he says. "Come on, I want to check out the new paintwork on your walls.

"Why?"

"Why? Because I want to make sure the painters did a good job."

"No, why did Romeo ask you to walk me home?"

"Because he couldn't be here to do it himself." He reaches around me and punches in the code for the building.

"How do you know that code?" I ask him.

"There might be one or two chicks in here who like late-night visits." He lifts his eyebrows up and down.

"Ah, gross." I screw up my nose and walk towards the stairs.

"You know, he really likes you, right," Luca says.

"Who?"

"Romeo, he likes you. And, well, he's never liked anyone before."

"Oh." What the hell am I supposed to say to that?

"I know you're a smart girl, Livvy. Where do you think the daughter of a cop and the son of a Valentino are destined to end up?"

"I don't know what you're talking about. I get it. You don't like me. I don't know why, considering I've never done anything to make you not like me. But I'm also used to not being liked. I'm not one of the cool kids. I'm not one of your cheerleading groupies."

"One, I like you plenty enough. What I don't like is the fact that you're going to break my brother's fucking heart and that's something he'll never recover from. And two, I don't have groupies."

"Why do you think I'm going to break his heart?"

"Because girls like you don't belong in our world, Livvy."

"Oh, so what's your mom like?" I ask him.

"She's the exception to the rule," he says, opening my dorm door and inviting himself in.

"Oh my god," I gasp, staring at my room. It's not a simple white paint cover-up job—the landlord's special as we call it—like I was expecting. It's a work of freaking art. There's a mural of flowers along the wall right next to my bed. And not just flowers. Lilies of the valley.

"Told you he likes you," Luca says before leaving the room, the door slamming behind him.

Chapter Thirteen

Romeo

"**D**id you walk her to her dorm?" I question Luca before lowering myself onto a balcony chair next to him. It's fucking freezing out here. Why he insists on sitting out in the cold, I'll never understand.

"You asked me to, didn't you?" he huffs.

I know what he's telling me. If I ask him to do something, he's going to do it. "How was she?"

"Here's an idea... why don't you pull your phone out of your pocket and your balls out of your ass, call her, and find out for yourself," he groans.

"What the fuck is your problem?"

"You are so fucking hung up on this girl, Romeo. It's fucking terrifying."

"Why?" I ask.

"Because I know you. I shared a goddamned womb with you and never have I seen you react this way to anyone."

"She's different." That's the only explanation I can give him. I don't know what is happening to me when it comes to Livvy. All I know is that she's *different*, and come hell or high water, she will be mine. She *is* mine.

"Yeah, what's going to happen when she breaks your heart?"

"That's not going to happen." I'd have to have a heart in order to have it broken.

"Yes, it is. Her father's a cop, Romeo. Do I really need to remind you who you are? Who our father is?"

"Ex-cop. I'll figure it out." I sigh. "Do you ever wish you were born into a different family? A normal one?"

"Sometimes I wonder what it'd be like to be free. But that's never gonna happen for us. We are Valentinos. There's no *out* for us."

"Not for me, but you've got an out. You're going pro. You'll move on to whatever team signs you."

"You think I'm going without you?" Luca laughs. "Wherever I go, you're coming."

"What if I don't?" I ask him. It was always our plan. To stick together. Whatever job I ended up doing for the family after college, I could do from whatever city Luca was signed to. But now I'm considering what Livvy will think of following Luca around the country. Which is beyond stupid. It doesn't matter what she thinks. If I go, I'm not about to leave her behind. At least that's what I'm telling myself to make myself not appear like such a fucking pussy. I'm not going to leave my brother high and dry, not for anyone. I'm also not going to lose Livvy—*fuck me, I haven't even had the girl yet and I'm planning our future together*.

"Then I won't go either." Luca shrugs.

"You'd stay here in New York because I wanted to?"

"Yes," he says, staring at the city skyline. It's his dream to play pro football. I have to figure out a way to make sure that happens for him. He's not giving that up for me.

"You know, whatever city we end up in will also need a prosecuting attorney." I smirk.

"Fuck me, I'm going to be the third wheel for the foreseeable future, aren't I?"

"You could try settling down? Find a nice girl. We could double date?" Even I want to throw up at that idea.

Luca's laugh is so loud I wouldn't be surprised if the whole city could hear it. "Yeah, that is not happening anytime soon, bro."

"I'm heading out," I tell him, pushing to my feet.

"You only just got here."

"Did you notice anything out of the ordinary when you walked Liv home?" I ask him.

"Like what?"

"Anyone lurking? She mentioned that she felt like she was being followed, then there was the vandalism."

"I didn't see anyone," he says.

I walk into my bedroom and pack an overnight bag. I don't plan on coming home tonight.

* * *

It's late. I know Livvy is more than likely asleep. I just need to see her. I need to be near her. Picking the lock of her dorm, I use my phone to light the path to her single bed. Where, sure enough, she is sound asleep. I look across to the other bed in the room to find it empty. Sandra isn't here and I thank my lucky stars that I have Livvy to myself. I know I'm creepy as I stand and watch her sleep. I just don't give a fuck. Kneeling down next to her, I gently push her hair away from her face. She stirs a little.

I lean over and pepper kisses on her forehead and her cheek, working my way to her ear. "Livvy, wake up," I whisper.

"Mmm, Romeo..." she murmurs, rolling over so she's flat on her back.

"Yeah, it's me," I reply.

109

Livvy's eyes pop open and she jolts up in bed. "Shit!" she screeches. "Romeo? What are you doing here?" Her gaze darts around the dark room.

"I wanted to see you," I tell her.

Livvy's stares at me for a moment. "How'd you get in here?"

"Ah, I might have picked your lock." I shrug and rise to my full height, toe off my boots, and then grab my shirt from the back of my neck and pull it off.

"Wait... what are you doing?"

"Well, I was planning on getting into bed with you and going to sleep, but I'm more than open to other suggestions if you have any," I tell her.

"Why?" she asks.

"Why what?"

"Why do you think you're getting into bed with me? I'm obviously dreaming, and this isn't really happening." Livvy pinches her arm.

"Not dreaming, babe, and I don't *think* I'm getting into bed with you. I *know* I am."

"Ah, nope. You can sleep in Sandra's bed. She's not here."

Yeah, that's *not* fucking happening. I don't plan on ever sleeping in another woman's bed again. However, I don't tell her that. I'm not purposely trying to scare her off. Without saying a word, I pull her covers back and squeeze into the bed. Livvy shuffles aside when I lie down. I wrap an arm around and pull her towards me, resting her head on my shoulder. Her body is stiff. I can feel her heart racing a million beats a minute.

"Relax, babe. We're just sleeping. I promise." My cock protests at my words. Feeling Livvy's body up against mine, I can't help but want more. I want to consume this girl. Mind, body, and soul.

"What's happening here, Romeo?" she asks in a soft voice, her tense muscles beginning to loosen.

"I don't want to sleep without you. I want to hold you in my arms all night," I tell her.

"Why?" she asks.

"Because you're mine."

Livvy is quiet. She doesn't say anything, her breathing is becoming more relaxed, and I think she's fallen back to sleep. As I lie here, staring into the darkened room, I have a strange sense of contentment wash over me. I've never been more comfortable in my own skin before. It's almost like Livvy is a calming balm to my soul. Which sounds corny as fuck, and you'd never hear me say those words out loud.

And then that calm turns to fear. Real, genuine fear. Because, for the first time in my life, I have something real to lose. Something other than my brothers or parents that my enemies can take away from me. Maybe I should talk to Pops. He'd know this feeling. He'd know what to do. He's managed to keep Mom safe all these years, although there have been a few close calls. My eyes close, I lean in, and my lips press against the top of Livvy's head. I inhale the fruity scent of her hair. This should be the red flag. I'm fucking sniffing her hair and enjoying it.

"If I'm yours, does that mean you're mine?" Livvy's voice breaks the silence.

"Every fiber of my being is yours," I tell her. I never thought I'd be able to give anyone anything. I didn't have anything to offer. I'm not worthy of Livvy, but I'm sure as fuck going to do my best to make myself worthy of her. I'm scared out of my mind that I'm not going to be enough, that Luca is right and this is all going to blow up in my face. One thing I've learned from my father is to always go after what you want in life and never let anyone tell you that you can't have it. Right now, the thing I want most is Livvy. I'm sure Pops wasn't talking about girls when he gave us those lectures, but I'm applying those lessons to this situation anyway.

"You're really big, so that's a lot of fibers. You don't even know me," Livvy says.

I laugh. It's a foreign feeling, being this at ease. "If I don't know you, then why the fuck am I so pulled to you? I feel like maybe I've known you in many lifetimes and this is just the beginning of a new beginning for us."

"And how does it end? Tragically, like Romeo and Juliet? Or happily ever after, like Elizabeth and Fitzwilliam?"

"Is that your way of proposing to me, Livvy? My answer is yes, by the way. Both of those couples ended up married. I would, however, have to go with Elizabeth and Fitzwilliam. I'd like more than a few hours of happiness with you."

"That most certainly wasn't a proposal, and you're very much against the sanctum of marriage, remember?"

"No, I'm not. I just said I haven't had a reason to believe in forever yet," I correct her.

"Mmm, forever is a really long time."

"Or it could be short," I say. In my family, today matters most. Tomorrow may or may not come for any of us.

"Romeo?"

"Yeah?"

"Thank you for my flowers," she whispers.

Chapter Fourteen

Livvy

My eyes pop open. I'm vividly aware of my surroundings. There is no slow consciousness seeping in. I don't think I've ever woken so suddenly, or been so alert. And it all has to do with the arm weighing me down, holding my back flush against a warm body.

A warm, hard body. A body that belongs to none other than Romeo Valentino. I guess it wasn't a dream

114

last night. Romeo really did come to my room. He really did climb into bed and he absolutely held me all night. My hips move on their own accord—that's the only explanation I can give for the fact that my ass is currently pressing against the hardness that can only be his cock. My thighs squeeze together. I feel wetness between them. My breathing picks up. I'm no virgin, but I've only ever been with Kirk. And, well, he certainly was nothing like Romeo. The guy is huge. And, by the feel of things, he's huge everywhere. I can't help but let my mind drift, imagining what it'd feel like to have him sliding into me.

This isn't me. I'm not the girl who jumps into boys' beds. I'm not overly sexual at all. I never really have been. I've also never been more turned on than I am right now. If I were a different girl, I'd probably roll over, grab that impressive appendage of his in my hands, and then... well, shit, I don't even know where to start with that dream.

A small moan escapes my mouth, and my hand flies up to cover it.

"If you keep grinding that hot little ass of yours on me, I'm not going to be responsible for what happens next, Livvy. I really am trying to be a gentleman here, babe." Romeo's husky voice vibrates right through me.

"What happens next?" I ask him, wanting nothing more than to find out the answer.

"Mmm, I'm not sure you're ready for that," he says.

I roll over to face him. "I think we're not living in

the 1700s, and you are certainly no gentleman like Mr. Darcy, so let's drop the pretenses and stop wasting time. If I say I want to know what happens next, then I want to know. So, Romeo, what exactly would happen next?" I ask more firmly. I don't proclaim to be overly feminist, but when anyone tells me what I'm thinking, or what I should or shouldn't do, the 'I am lady, hear me roar' part of me just rushes out to prove them all wrong.

Romeo's eyes widen in shock. Shit, did I overdo the roar? You know what? I don't care. Screw him if he thinks he can come in here and tell me what I am or *am not* ready for.

"What would happen next?" He repeats my question. "First, I'd roll you over, lay you flat on your back. I'd kiss you, but not gentle and soft like you deserve, because I'm fucking starving for a taste of you. I've been dreaming of how it would feel to kiss you. Then I'd let my hand wander up your legs. I'd slide your panties to the side and be pleasantly surprised to find your pussy soaking wet for me. I'd glide my fingers up your slit, circle your clit, before shoving them into your tight little hole. I'd make you come on my hand, and when you thought you couldn't possibly take anymore, I'd rip those panties off and replace my fingers with my cock. I'd bury myself so deep inside you that my cock leaves a permanent imprint."

By the time he finishes talking, I'm on my back and Romeo is hovering above me, his lips millimeters from my mine. My chest heaves up and down as my breathing increases. "That, I want that," I manage to get out.

Romeo lifts his head, tilting it to the side, his eyes searing right through mine. "Are you sure?" he asks.

"Where and what time thou wilt perform the rite, and all my fortunes at thy foot I'll lay. And follow thee, my lord, throughout the world." I don't know if he will understand the meaning of my quote. But just how loud of a yes can I yell?

Yes, I'm sure. And, yes, I've never been more certain of anything in my life.

"You have bewitched me, body and soul." Romeo quotes the words of Mr. Darcy right before he leans in and his lips fuse with mine. I feel like I'm floating, which is ridiculous, because I have a six-foot-something solid wall of muscle on top of me. My arms wrap around his neck, tugging him closer. Romeo runs his tongue along the seam of my lips. And the moment they part for him, his tongue delves in. "Mmm, so fucking perfect," he says, pulling back slightly before his hand cups my chin and tilts my head. His tongue plunges inside my mouth again.

I get lost in him. I can't believe I'm kissing Romeo Valentino. Technically, he's kissing me, which is even better. My legs wrap around his waist, tightening and pulling him as close as I can. If I could embed myself into his skin right now, I would. His hand grips my left thigh before he lifts his body, creating a small space between us. His kiss deepens, and his words ring true. There is nothing gentle about it. It's rough. Carnal. Pure lust and need.

His fingers trail up the inside of my thigh. My legs open wider, giving him easier access to where I really want those fingers to be. Romeo pushes my panties to the side, sliding his fingers between my wet folds. If it weren't for his tongue jammed down my throat right now, I'd be screaming out in pleasure. His kiss swallows all of my sounds. My hips buck up towards him as his fingers circle around my hardened bud. And I swear I see stars. I'm seconds away from coming and he's only just touched me. My hands tangle in his hair, tugging at the strands. I don't know if I'm trying to pull him away or towards me at this point.

I'm lost to the pleasure his talented fingers are wringing from my body. How can he so effortlessly bring me to nothing but a wanton mess? Is this what sex is supposed to feel like? Because I've never felt like this before, and this isn't even sex. This is a heavy make-out session. Romeo inserts one finger in my dripping center, curling it up and rubbing against a hidden spot I didn't know existed.

"Oh, hell, Romeo, don't stop," I moan out as my hips buck up, pressing into his hand.

"Non lo farò mai." *Never going to*, he says. And the next thing I know, my vision blurs as pleasure upon pleasure runs through my body like a wildfire. It's like a never-ending orgasm. It just keeps coming—well, I just keep coming. When I finally return to earth, my body wrecked with aftershocks, Romeo is dragging my ruined panties down my legs. "So fucking pretty," he says, looking directly at my exposed, bare pussy. His tongue darts out and licks his bottom lip. "Are you sure you want this, Liv? Because once we do this, you will be mine," he asks.

I'm not sure if he's giving me an out or just trying to be a gentleman. Whatever the case, at this point in time, I can't think of anything I'd rather do. If he can pull that kind of pleasure from me with just his fingers, imagine what he could do with his cock.

I nod my head. "I'm sure. Make me yours, Romeo."

"Just so we're clear," Romeo says, leaning over the bed and reaching for something on the floor. When he straightens up again, he's ripping into a foil wrapper. "You were already mine, whether we did this or not." My eyes stay transfixed on him. He's pulled his black boxers down and is rolling the condom on his shaft. On his extremely huge fucking shaft. So huge that I'm suddenly having second thoughts. "Livvy, have you done this before?" he asks me.

"Yes."

His face hardens. I don't think he likes that answer; however, I'm not about to lie. "But that," I say, pointing at his cock. "I don't think that's going to fit, and I know how stupid that sounds but have you seen yourself, Romeo? It's huge."

Romeo smirks and I wish I had a camera to capture

his face in this moment. It's carefree, proud, lustful, happy. All the emotions I've come to learn are a rare find with this man. "Thanks. But trust me, nothing is going to stop me from sinking into you." He lines his tip up with my entrance. Leaning over my body, he enters me slowly, stretching me completely. I may not be a virgin, but my sexual experience is limited to one boy. And, well, there is nothing boyish about Romeo. Once he's fully seated, he leans in and whispers in my ear, "I may not be your first, Livvy, but I'll make sure I'm your last and you'll never remember any who came before me."

My legs wrap around his waist, my arms around his neck, and I hold him close to me as he starts to move in and out of me. Gently. "Romeo, faster," I tell him. He sits back, picking up my left leg and resting my ankle on his shoulder, and thrusts forward again. "Oh god!" My head falls to the side and my eyes close.

"Open your eyes. I want you to see who's fucking you, Livvy. I want you to know that it's me, and only me," Romeo grunts as he increases his speed. I pry my eyes open and connect them with his. It's so hard not to look away, not to hide from whatever huge connection is happening between the two of us. "Fuck, I knew you'd feel good but this is something else. Your pussy is fucking perfect. And mine." His thrusts become more erratic, harder, faster.

"I'm going to..." I don't finish my sentence as my

whole body seizes up, and a hurricane of tingling pleasure rips through me.

"Yes, squeeze my cock. So. Fucking. Good," he says as he empties himself. Romeo falls on top of me. We're both fighting to catch our breath. Picking his head up, he smiles down at me. "Please tell me we can do that again, because I think I might just die if I never get to feel your pussy choking my cock again."

I laugh. "Who knew you were such a sweet talker?"

"I'll be anything you want me to be if you let me do that."

"Mmm, I think that can be arranged." I smile, reach up, bring his face down to mine, and lose myself in his kiss.

Chapter Fifteen

Romeo

I wonder if it's too late to change majors? I don't like not being in the same classes as Livvy. I hated leaving her this morning when she had to go. The only consolation is she agreed to meet me in the cafeteria for lunch. Which is where I find myself now. Waiting for her. Every time the door opens, my eyes scan the students entering. I look at my watch for the hundredth time. She's not late.

Ten minutes past the time we said we'd meet isn't late. Is it?

Fucking hell, I just need to lay my eyes on her. I need to know she's okay. Maybe I should text her...

"You need to take a fucking chill pill, bro. Relax. She'll be here."

"I'm relaxed," I tell Luca through gritted teeth.

"Sure you are." He laughs, throwing a fry at my face.

"How do you know she'll be here?" I ask him —*pathetic, I know.*

"Because, for some unknown reason, she likes you." He shrugs.

"You like me," I remind him.

"You're my brother, my twin. I kind of have to like you."

"Nope, you could like Theo or Matteo more than me, but I'm your favorite brother," I remind him.

"Again, twin. Also, Theo? Really, if anyone was in the running to take your place as favorite, it'd be Matteo. At least he knows how to have a good time," Luca says.

"You think Theo would be different if he didn't have to take over? I mean, it can't be easy trying to follow in Pops's footsteps."

"Pops isn't going anywhere anytime soon, and Theo just needs to relax and pull that stick out of his grumpy old ass."

"Fuck, I hope we never get that grumpy when we're as old as he is."

"Never. We'll always be fun. Well, I'll be fun and you'll be with me so that counts," Luca says.

The door opens again and I finally let out the breath I didn't know I was holding. Livvy walks in and looks around the cafeteria. She seems flustered. When she finds where we're sitting, she walks over and takes the chair next to me. "Sorry I'm late. I forgot a textbook I need for my next class and had to run back to my dorm," she says, avoiding eye contact with me.

Luca leans over the table, his gaze narrowed at Livvy. "Who the fuck made you cry?" he growls.

My head snaps to the side. Taking Livvy's chin in my hand, I turn her face around until she's looking at me. She peers up at me with wide eyes. "I'm fine," she says, trying to bat my hand away.

"You've been crying. What happened?" I ask, my voice calm.

"I haven't. I just have really bad hay fever."

"In winter? Doubtful," I tell her. Leaning down, I meld my lips with hers. I kiss her like I can take away all of her worries. Whatever has upset her, I'll fix it. I pull away and she blinks her eyes back open. "Want to try again? What happened?"

"I... it's nothing. I'm fine. Let's just drop it. Please," she pleads with me.

I really don't want to drop it. Not at all. But I can tell this isn't something she wants to talk about right now. "This conversation isn't over," I grunt, my hand falling away from her chin.

"Fucking whore!"

I hear the words right before a tray comes flying in Livvy's direction. My arm reaches around her, deflecting the projectile. Luca is on his feet within seconds while I'm shoving Livvy behind me. "What the fuck did you just say?" I yell at the pathetic cheerleader standing in front of me.

"I didn't stutter, Romeo. You know, if you're going to fuck around on me, at least have the decency to do it in private."

Luca's laugh echoes through the now-quiet cafeteria. "Oh my god! You have got to be fucking kidding me."

"Shut up, Luca, I wasn't talking to you." The girl, whose name I can't fucking recall, hisses at him.

"No, you were just leaving and taking your crazy with you," my twin fires back at her.

"Come on, Romeo, you can't seriously be this stupid," the chick directs at me before looking around my shoulder to Livvy. "Honey, do yourself a favor and walk away now before you embarrass yourself any further. This little game Romeo likes to play with girls is getting old. Don't think you're the first and you won't be the last either. Just know that when he's done with you, he'll come running back to me." She smirks.

"What fucking drugs are you on?" I hiss at her.

"Romeo, I'm gonna go. I'll, uh…" Livvy doesn't

finish her sentence. She turns around and starts walking towards the entrance.

"I would think very carefully about what leaves those lips next, because I won't hold him back when he guts you alive," Luca growls at the chick—*again, I have no idea what her fucking name is.*

I don't bother to stick around. Instead, I run off to catch up with Livvy. Fuck me, I can feel God laughing at my ass now. He gave me something precious, and of course he's not going to let me keep her. It was too fucking good to be true. Maybe I should just cut my losses now.

Fuck that. Nope, Livvy's mine. No matter what anyone says.

"Livvy, wait up." I catch up with her outside the cafeteria. Wrapping my hand around her elbow, I spin her around to face me. Fucking hell, she's crying. Tears fall from her eyes, each one cutting into a soul I didn't even think I had. "Please don't cry. I don't know who the fuck that girl is."

"It doesn't matter. We're not... I'm not... I can't do this, Romeo."

"You can't do what?" I ask.

"This." Livvy points between the two of us. "It shouldn't have happened. We don't run in the same circles. We're not compatible."

"Well, it felt like we were pretty fucking compatible this morning, Liv. It's too late anyway. This is happening. We are happening," I tell her.

126

"Do you really think that girls like her are going to be our biggest hurdle? You're, well, you... I'm sure there will be plenty of girls just like her. But that I can deal with. What about our families, Romeo? What do you really think my dad is going to do when he finds out who you are and what we are?"

"We are endgame. That's what we are, Livvy." I wrap my arm around her shoulders and pull her up against my chest. "I don't care who they are. I won't let anyone take you from me, Livvy, not even you."

"That's... I need to show you something," she says, pulling away from me. I watch silently as she draws her phone from her pocket. Pressing a few buttons, she turns it around to show me a text.

UNKNOWN:

> He can't always be with you. I'll wait for the right time to pounce, little mouse.

I read the message, and my vision blurs. I don't even hear Luca approach us, not until he looks over my shoulder and starts cursing in Italian.

What the fuck is this? "When did you get this?" I ask aloud.

"Just before I left my last class."

"And you didn't come straight to me?"

"I thought... I don't know. I was scared, okay?" she yells.

"Shh, it's fine. You're okay, I'm not going to let

127

anything happen to you," I say, tugging her against me again. This is where she should always be. "Luca, get Marx and Adrian here. I have some shit to do and I'm not leaving Livvy home alone."

"Already on it," he says, tapping away at his phone.

We walk over to the parking lot and I place Livvy on the front passenger seat. "Who are Marx and Adrian?" she asks.

"Our friends," I tell her. I don't think the word *soldier* is really what she needs to hear right now. I know she's not stupid. She's Googled me. She knows who my family is. I'm just not completely ready to face the reality that we do really come from two different stratospheres. Us being together never should have happened. But it did. So the world can burn down around us before I'll ever let it—or anyone—separate us.

Chapter Sixteen

Livvy

As much as I'm trying to focus on the text in front of me, I can't. My mind keeps drifting to Romeo. I slept in his bed last night. Alone. I don't know where he went. I don't know when he came home. But when I woke up, there was a note from him on the bedside table, telling me he'd see me this afternoon for our tutoring session. Luca made me breakfast, told me that Romeo had to go home and see their parents about something. Although he didn't elaborate more than that.

I'm worried. He hasn't texted, called, or emailed me all day. I don't want to be the needy girlfriend who has to know where he is at all times.

Shit. No. Not girlfriend.

I am *not* Romeo Valentino's girlfriend. Am I?

I mean, he says I'm *his*. But what does that really mean? I have no idea. We haven't discussed labels. Is it too early for that talk?

It's too early. It has to be.

I look back down at the text in front of me. I can't believe I'm even thinking like this. I need to concentrate. A pretty boy is not going to make me lose focus on what I want in life. Even if he does look like an Adonis and has moves that should be illegal. I get about five minutes of reading and highlighting done before a body fills the chair next to me. I smile. I don't need to look up to know that it's Romeo. I can smell his woodsy scent, and the anxiety I was feeling moments ago is gone, replaced by an eerie calm. The saying "if it's too good to be true, then it probably is" repeats in the back of my mind.

"Miss me?" he asks.

"Were you gone?" I smile up at him. I swear his beauty takes me by surprise every time I see him.

"Funny. If lawyering doesn't work out for you, there's always stand-up, right?"

"Always. A girl has to keep her options open, you know," I tell him.

He squints his eyes at me. "When it comes to careers, the world is your oyster, babe. You can be whatever you want to be. However, when it comes to boyfriends, those options are closed. Very fucking closed."

"Boyfriends? Are you saying you want to be my boyfriend, Romeo?"

"We've already had this conversation. I told you, you are mine." He leans in and seals his words with a kiss.

"We didn't put labels on anything," I remind him, pulling back from his mouth. As much as I want to climb onto him and take things further, we're in the library.

Romeo's lips tilt up at one side. "You want a label, Liv? Like, girlfriend? Because that doesn't really seem like enough. We can skip all the labels and go straight to wife, you know. I can have the Valentino jet ready to fly us to Vegas in an hour. Just say the word."

I laugh because he has to be joking. At least I hope he is... I don't think he is, but I'm going to pretend it's a joke because that is not a can of worms I'm willing to open right now. "I think I'd like to experience all the titles. No need to skip any."

"Girlfriend it is then, for now."

"Why do I feel like you're going to break my heart, Romeo?"

"I break a lot of things, Liv, but you will never be one of them. I promise."

His words are so sincere I have to fight the tears from falling. How can he know exactly what I need to hear? How can he be so damn perfect?

"We should study. You're not going to get that essay done if we keep chitchatting away your study hours."

"I have a better idea," he says, standing and holding out a hand.

"What?"

"Come with me." He takes my palm and pulls me up.

I go to grab my bag, my books, and Romeo stops me. "Leave them there. They'll be fine. Marx will make sure no one touches anything."

A man steps out of nowhere, a big beefy man in a suit. My throat goes dry. How long has he been there? I remember Romeo talking to Luca about Marx and Adrian last night, but I never saw them. If there was ever a uniform for the mafia, Marx would be wearing it. It's so easy to forget about Romeo's family when I'm with him. He dresses so casually, usually in a pair of jeans and a t-shirt. But staring at the big beefy man in a black suit in front of me, I'm instantly reminded of exactly who Romeo Valentino is. But is that enough to stop me from following him to God only knows where?

Not even close.

I end up in a private study room. As soon as we

step through the door, Romeo has me pinned up against the door. His lips are hungrily devouring mine as he picks me up from the back of my thighs. My legs wrap around his waist, and my fingers tangle in his hair as he grinds his hardness right onto my clit.

"Fuck, I missed you. I fucking need you so much," he grunts before his mouth travels down my neck. He nibbles on one spot, a particular spot that has my spine arching and moans escaping from my mouth.

"Please." I'm not sure what I'm asking for—yes, I am. I'm asking for pleasure I know he can deliver.

"Please what? What do you want?" Romeo asks.

"I want you."

"Be more specific? You want me how? You want my fingers? My mouth? My cock? What exactly do you want, Liv?"

I can feel the blush rise up on my neck, crawling it's way to my face as I think about having his mouth on me. That's something I've never experienced. As curious as I am, I don't want to do that here. We shouldn't be doing *anything* here. Still, I find myself telling him, "I want your cock, Romeo. I want you."

"You have me, more than you know." He sets me down on my feet and then spins me around so my front is pressed up against the door. I feel Romeo's heat at my back as he steps as close as he can to me. His hands lift my skirt up to my waist before I hear a rip—the sound of my panties being torn. Guess I didn't really need them anyway. "You have no idea how much I've been dreaming of getting back into this pussy of yours. I don't just want it. I fucking need it," he grunts.

I turn my head to see him undoing his jeans. He takes out his cock, pumping it a few times. The sight makes my mouth water. I want to taste him. I don't know if I'd be any good at pleasuring him like that, but I sure would give it my best shot. Romeo pulls a foil packet out of his back pocket. "Are you always prepared?" I ask with a raised brow.

"If you were dating you, you'd always be prepared to fuck too, babe," he says, rolling the rubber down over his shaft.

I'm not complaining. I'm glad one of us is thinking sensibly enough about safety because I honestly would have let him fuck me without one. I just want to feel him inside me. I want to come. He says he's been dreaming of it. I doubt he's thought about it as much as I have though. I made myself come in his bed last night, but even that wasn't anywhere near as good as the ecstasy I know he can give.

"Brace yourself, babe. This is going to be rough and quick," he warns before lining his cock up with my entrance and slamming inside me.

"Oh god, hell, Romeo," I cry out and his hand comes up to cover my mouth.

"I fucking love hearing your screams, but I don't share well, and your pleasure is not something I'm ever going to share. Those screams are mine; your moans are mine." He thrusts into me. Harder. Faster. His other hand wraps around the front of my hips, and his fingers find my clit and rub circles on the hardened bud.

I'm seconds away from combusting, but he knows that. Of course he does. "Romeo, I'm going to... shit." My words are muffled by the palm currently covering my mouth.

"That's it. Come for me, Livvy. Soak my fucking cock with your juices. I want it all," he grunts into my ear. "You feel so fucking good."

His teeth bite down on my earlobe, and the pain radiates throughout my whole body, quickly transforming to pleasure. The kind I've only ever experienced with Romeo before. My legs tremble. He catches me, his arm wrapping around my waist and propping me up as he finishes. His thrusts are wild as he empties inside me. Romeo pulls out and spins me around, pressing my back against the door. His lips slam down on mine, and his tongue delves in, tangling with my own. By the time he pulls back again, I'm breathless.

"That was...." I'm at a loss for words as to how to describe it.

"Fucking brilliant." Romeo smirks. "You're fucking perfect. Don't ever change," he says, pecking me on the lips again.

Chapter Seventeen

Romeo

I send Livvy a message to let her know I'll see her later tonight. It's Friday, fight night for my and Luca's underground club. Walking into the garage, I find my twin warming up at the bag. He stops when he spots me, picking up a towel from the ground before making his way over.

"You're late," he says.

"I had shit to do."

"You had Livvy to do." He doesn't see the fist I send his way, my knuckles immediately connecting with his jaw. Luca smirks at me, rubbing at his face. "Did I hit a nerve?"

"Don't fucking disrespect her," I growl at him. I love my brother. I'd give my own life for any of my siblings, but fuck if I'll ever let them disrespect Livvy.

"I wasn't. I was disrespecting *you*, asshole. Her, I like. You, not so much lately."

"Sure you don't." I laugh.

The thing with Luca and me is, whenever we argue, we are always quick to move past it. To come back to being us. Two against the world.

"So, what were you doing?"

"Showering. You should try it sometime, might help you pick up a girl worth bringing home to Ma," I tell him.

"Why the fuck would I want to do that?" He screws up his face at the thought of settling down. "Wait... are you taking Livvy to family dinner on Sunday?"

"Fuck no, and you're not saying shit about her to anyone," I warn him. I need to make her fall in love with me before I introduce her to the fucking psychopaths in my family. It's not just my immediate family either. There're my aunts and uncles, cousins... Jesus, my cousin Izzy alone is enough to scare the devil himself away. Livvy is not ready for that yet. And I'm not ready to lose her, which means keeping her away from the rest of the Valentinos as much as possible.

"My lips are sealed. You know I've always got your back, bro," Luca reminds me.

"Thanks. So who's the fool who thinks he can beat you tonight?" I ask.

"Jacob Kinsley." He smiles wide.

"The fucking baseball captain? What the fuck is he doing fighting?"

"No idea, but who am I to turn down a fair fight?" Luca shrugs his shoulders.

"There's nothing fair about it. Don't do permanent damage, Luc. That's the man's career. It's not like he has anything else going for him." The fucking loser is as dumb as they come. If he weren't so good at baseball, no amount of his parents' money would have gotten him into this school.

"Contrary to popular belief, I'm not an animal. I do have some degree of self-control," Luca says.

I raise an eyebrow at him. We both know he has no such thing. I don't need to say the words, because he knows what I'm thinking. "You and self-control have no relationship at all."

Luca shakes his head and walks over to Henry, who is setting up his little desk in the corner. "How we looking?"

"You're looking like you two can retire and never work another day in your life. With tonight's fight, you're at a total of one million, four hundred thousand. Give or take," Henry says.

"Nobody retires off a million dollars," Luca counters with a roll of his eyes.

"Normal people actually do. Lots and lots of them," Henry replies.

"Are you saying we're not normal?" I ask him.

"Ah, well... yes, that's what I'm saying. Normal people don't drive around in five hundred thousand dollar cars at our age."

I'll have you know I earned that car. Every cent of it.

Working for the family businesses isn't exactly child's play. These are the words I don't say out loud though. The number one rule in my family is you don't talk about the family. Especially our businesses. You don't acknowledge the rumors that our father is the head of the Valentino Crime Family—fuck, you don't acknowledge that there *is* a Valentino Crime Family. To my knowledge, my father is a businessman, a ruthless but legal one. That's all that anyone who doesn't know better needs to know at all.

I'm aware Livvy has read the articles, and that she knows the rumors. Does she believe them? If so, why the fuck hasn't she asked me about them yet? She made that one mafia prince comment, but that seemed more in jest. And, more importantly, what the fuck am I going to tell her when she does?

* * *

An hour later, the garage is packed to the rafters, the crowd roaring as Luca and his opponent go jab for jab in the cage. The door opens and the last two people I want to see right now walk in. Our brothers. Theo and Matteo. They spot me immediately and make a beeline for where I'm standing. Theo looks pissed. I mean, he always *looks* pissed, but now more so than I've seen him in a while.

"What the fuck do you Wonder Twins think you're doing here?" he growls at me.

"Ah, well, I'm watching a fight? What are you two doing here?" I ask him.

"Don't be an ass, Romeo. What's he doing in that fucking cage? Shut it the fuck down. Now."

"Can't do that until he wins. Sorry, bro." I shrug.

Theo draws the pistol from behind his back. Holding it in the air, he pulls the trigger. The sound echoes off the walls, and the whole garage goes silent, right before everyone starts screaming and running for the door.

"Was that really necessary?" I ask.

"Yes, you two in the fucking car now." Theo gestures to me and then Luca, who is standing in the cage huffing and puffing from exhaustion.

"Why? I'm a little busy tonight. I have plans," I tell him.

"Well, now your only plans are coming with me.

I'm not going to fucking ask again, Romeo. Get your shit. We're leaving."

Usually I would argue with him more. However, when it comes to dealing with a Valentino, you really do need to know when you *can* and *can't* win an argument—as well as when it's worth even *trying*. And I can tell that this is not one of those times. Theo and Matteo didn't come out here on their own accord. This has Pops written all over it. He's found out Luca's been fighting and is more than likely fucking pissed that his star player son is being so reckless with his body. I'm surprised we've lasted this long without our old man stepping in. Nothing happens in this city without his knowledge, especially when it comes to us kids. So the fact that we've gone a few months before getting shut down is a feat in itself.

"You know, it really was nice knowing you while it lasted. Don't worry, bro, I'll make sure I look fucking great at your funeral." Matteo laughs at his own lame-ass joke.

"Do you know a plastic surgeon skilled enough to help you, because short of a miracle, no amount of designer threads will make you look anywhere close to great, Matteo," I retort.

He blinks at me with a blank face. "You do know we're brothers. We share the same DNA; we're the same. You didn't insult me. You insulted yourself, you fucking moron."

"Yeah, read a textbook sometime. That's not how DNA works. We are not the same."

"You're right. We're not. I'm much cooler." He smirks before heading out to the car.

Luca and I share a look as we stalk out behind them. "You know I have my car here. I can follow you," I tell Theo.

"Nice try. I don't have all night to chase you two fuckwits around the city. Get in. I'll have your cars picked up," he says, putting a stop to my attempt at making a break for it.

Sitting in the back seat of Theo's car, I send Livvy a message. I know I'm not going to be seeing her tonight.

ME:

> Sorry, babe, a family thing came up. I won't make it to your place this weekend.

I get a response immediately.

LIVVY:

> Are you okay? It's probably a good thing you're not meeting me here. I have so much studying to catch up on anyway.

Are you okay? I'm missing out on spending a night with her. So, no, I'm not fucking okay. It's such a simple question. It shouldn't have so much effect on me that she even asked it. Of course she'd ask something like that. She's fucking nice. That's what nice people do.

Me:

You're the smartest person I know. You don't need to study. I'll see you Sunday. Call me if you need anything.

LIVVY:

Okay. xx

* * *

Luca and I share another look, one that tells the other to keep their mouth shut and we might make it out of here alive. We've just been hand-delivered to our parents' house, after being stuck with Theo all weekend, to ensure we don't miss Sunday night's dinner. Something Mom will not let any of the Valentino boys miss often.

"Didn't I tell you two you had to stop growing? What are they feeding you on campus?" Mom wraps Luca in a hug, kissing his cheek before moving on to me. Her arms go around me, squeezing tight. "It's been too long," she says.

"Ma, you saw us last Sunday." I laugh.

"And it feels like a lifetime, Romeo." Her eyes inspect mine, searching for God only knows what. "I don't know what you two did, but remember we love you always, no matter what." With that, she turns

143

around and walks down the hall. "Oh, and your father's waiting for you in his study. Theo, follow me," she calls out over her shoulder.

"Don't worry, I'll make sure to spend both of your shares of inheritance on hookers and strippers. It's what you would have done anyway." Matteo laughs, following Luca and me into our father's office.

I know my old man. He's intimidating. I've seen him in action, and let's just say the fact that he can still sleep at night after the things he's done is a damn miracle. Am I scared of him though?

Not even in the slightest. He might yell, throw something or even go for a slap across the back of the head. But we're his sons. There is nothing more important to him than family. Well, making Mom happy has always been his number one priority in life. It just so happens that our mother loves us a whole lot, so to keep her happy, he needs to keep us alive.

My twin and I share a wordless conversation. "*Do not crack under pressure*," we each tell the other without actually saying anything. I don't know how we do it, but we've always been able to just *know* what the other is thinking. We stand in front of his desk. Pops doesn't look up at us; instead, he continues reading through whatever paperwork he is scanning. When he does glance our way, I realize he was probably just counting to ten in his head to try to stay calm.

"Do you have any idea how fucking stupid the two of you are?" he yells, glaring at me and then Luca.

We side-eye each other. Smirking, I turn back to Pops. "Well, if we knew how stupid we were, Pops, we probably wouldn't be stupid, now, would we?" I duck just in time to avoid the stapler that's aimed where my head was.

Pops's finger points at me, then my twin, and then back to me again. "It stops now. There will be no more underground fighting empires in this family." That finger moves over to Luca. "And you will not get involved with any fights at all, you hear me. You're fucking lucky you can still throw at all after the bullet you took last year."

Pops ain't wrong. My brother got shot last year at our cousin Lily's house in Australia. Some fuckers thought they could break in and attack her. We weren't about to let anyone get to her. Pops hasn't gotten over that incident yet. You'd think as a Don of the most ruthless fucking crime family in New York, he'd be able to handle seeing one of his own kids take a bullet. But, no, he's more protective than Mom sometimes. And that's saying something because our mother is the very definition of an angry momma bear.

"What do you think your mother is going to say if she finds out about this stunt of yours?" he asks, rubbing his temples.

"Wasn't planning on her finding out, Pops," Luca says.

I turn and glare at Theo and Matteo, who are

laughing their asses off behind us. When did Theo sneak in?

"You really are fucking dimwits, aren't you? You still think you can hide shit from her? Well, it's your funeral," Theo grunts.

"Come on, Pops, it was just a few fights. No one got hurt," I try to reason with our father.

Theo slaps me across the back of the head, at the same time Pops says, "Tell that to the guys being wheeled out on gurneys."

"Ah, what the fuck?" I growl at Theo.

"Do you two really think I have nothing better to do than come and bail your asses out of shit every other fucking day? Start smarting the fuck up." Theo stomps over to the wet bar—*someone got up on the wrong side of the fucking bed this morning.*

"Dinner's ready!" Mom's voice rings out through the intercom on the wall, like a saving grace. And Luca and I practically bolt from the room. Dinner is the very best excuse to get out of any further interrogations.

"This conversation isn't over, you two," Pops calls from behind us.

"Yes, boss," Luca and I say together.

Chapter Eighteen

Livvy

I know I shouldn't be pining for Romeo right now, but I am. Somehow, in the last couple of weeks, I've let him creep under my skin to the point that I'm missing him. Which is stupid. I barely know him. Well, I know how good he is at handing out orgasms, and he's super attentive and passionate about whatever it is we discuss. I know that he's a lot brighter than he lets on. I also know that whatever is keeping him away this weekend can't be good.

He did message me on Friday, saying a family thing came up. Is that family thing just the weekly dinner he told me that his mom makes them all attend? I really do hope that's all it is.

Deciding that I'm not going to get much studying done tonight, I pack up my books. I was planning on sitting in the library until I got kicked out. Sandra is staying at her parents' place until tomorrow, and I didn't feel like being stuck in the dorm room alone. I'm alone here too, but I'm also surrounded by other students. And it's not as lonely. Walking out the library doors, I pull my coat closed tighter and hitch my backpack up on my right shoulder.

It's getting colder and colder. I'm not used to such cold winters. Back home it was cold, but not like this. The icy wind chills me to the bone. Or is it the feeling that I'm being followed? Watched? I crane my neck around, but I can't see anyone. I need to remember to thank my father for making me so paranoid all the time. My pace quickens. I have just a few more minutes, a few more steps, before I reach my dorm. As soon as I'm inside, I'll be fine. This anxiety, fear, it will ease once I'm passed those doors. I can see the building and immediately start to relax. That's until I hear thudding footsteps approaching from behind me. I turn around and freeze as a pair of hands swipe out and grab me. One covers my mouth, while the other holds the back of my head.

"Don't scream. Don't fight. And this will all be over very quickly for you," a thick Russian accent says. I kick out. I don't care how big this guy is. I'm not going down without a fight. My dad taught me self-defense. Yet, in this moment, when I really need those skills, I've got nothing. As my foot connects with his shin, another pair of arms grabs me from behind, lifting me off the ground.

"Stop! Help!" I scream the moment my mouth is uncovered. My arms and legs are flailing to no avail. I'm dragged behind a building, into the shadows, where I'm forced to the ground. I know the grass is cold. Damp. But I can't feel it. I can't think about anything but getting away.

Get up, Livvy. Do not let them do this. My inner voice is telling me I need to fight.

Using all my strength, I struggle against them. The fingers digging into my skin. The limbs bearing down on me. I thrash and attempt to connect with anything solid. Something hard strikes my temple, and then my arms are grabbed and tugged above my head. Tears roll down my cheeks. There are two of them. One holding my wrists, the other straddling my legs. No matter how much I fight, try to buck this guy off me, it's no use. I'm not strong enough. But I'm also not going to give up. I scream until my throat is hoarse. I try to call for help. This only serves to gain me a backhand across the face.

My head snaps to the side, and a metallic taste fills my mouth.

It doesn't stop me from fighting though. "Get off. Please don't do this. Please." I resort to begging, although I can already tell it won't work.

"Fucking shut the fuck up, bitch." The man on top hisses into my face. Another Russian accent. I stare at him. Take in every detail I can make out. He has a scar across his right cheek. My continued struggles are getting me nowhere. When his fingers reach for the button on my jeans, I scream as loud as I can.

A hand reaches out and pulls on my hair, forcing my head to roll backwards. "Shut the fuck up," the man behind me says, right before his closed fist connects with my nose. My vision blurs, and I fight to not let the blackness take over.

I don't know if it's been seconds or minutes, but my eyes snap open right as an extreme, sharp pain radiates up my core. "Please, stop," I cry out. My voice is weak.

He doesn't stop. He continues to use my body for his own sick pleasure, smirking down at me throughout his assault. There's nothing I can do. I have never felt more helpless in my life. I'm left with no choice but to lie here and hope that this is over soon. I need this to be over soon.

I'm not this girl. I'm not the victim. Except, I am. And the worst bit is that no matter how much I fight, I can't get myself out of this situation. The man pulls out of me, and I feel liquid spill all over my stomach. The sounds of his grunted finale make me turn my head and vomit all over the grass.

"Fucking sick bitch," he says, standing. And I lie there and watch as he walks away.

"Next time, I'll make sure it's my turn," a voice hisses from above my head.

My eyes roll up and I can just make out his bright-blue irises before he follows his co-conspirator into the shadows. I don't know how long it takes but I finally manage to pull myself up off the ground. I need to get into my dorm. Everything hurts as I slide my jeans back up my legs. I don't bother to fasten them as I search for my bag in the grass, the contents of which have tumbled out and spread across the lawn. After scooping it all up, I stumble to the back door of my dorm.

I just need to get inside. Once I'm inside, I'll be okay. Hopefully. I close myself in my dorm room and allow the sobs to rack my whole body. I sink to the floor as the events that just took place really hit home. I was... I can't even say the word in my head. I don't know what to do. What are you supposed to do after this happens to you?

I need to get clean. I need to wash them off me. I pull myself up and walk into the bathroom. I avoid looking in the mirror, too afraid of who will be looking back at me. Turning the shower on as hot as it will go, I peel my clothes from my body and step under the water. I can see marks and bruising already forming.

There's dried blood between my legs. I snatch the bodywash from the shelf, grab the loofah, and soap up my skin. It's not enough though. I repeat the process, doing my best to scrub their touch from me.

After the entire bottle is empty, I still don't feel clean. The water has gone cold, so I shut it off and wrap a towel around me. I change into a pair of sweats and a shirt before I crawl under my covers and let myself fall apart. Everything hurts. I try to close my eyes but they snap back open. All I can see is his face, the scar running down his cheek. I can still hear the groans, their voices, the thick accent.

I spend the entire night tossing and turning. Thankfully Sandra didn't show up at the dorm this morning. I should take myself somewhere else, a hotel. If only I could afford it. I thought about calling home. I really want my dad right now. But I don't. If I do that, then I'll never be allowed to return. He will come and make me go home, probably after he does something that will ruin the rest of his life. And I can't let that happen. I won't let what happened to me impact anyone else. I just need to make sure no one ever finds out.

* * *

I must fall asleep at some point. Because I wake to a loud banging on the door. My first thought is *they're back*. They've come back for me.

I pull the cover up over my head. I know it's stupid. It's not going to save me, but if I can block the world out, maybe it will all go away.

Then I hear it. His voice. Romeo. I can't let him see me like this...

Chapter Nineteen

Romeo

Where is she? Livvy's never late. Her Monday sessions just happened to open up, so of course I booked those too. And in the four weeks she's been my tutor, she always arrives before me. Or at least that's what I let her think. I've been standing here, in the dark corner of the library where I usually watch her, for the last thirty minutes. My knee bounces. Something isn't right. My gut is twisting, my mind racing with a thousand scenarios of what could have happened. None of them fucking good. Call it an occupational hazard, always expecting the worst. I can't sit here and wait any longer. I need to go find her.

Pushing off the wall, I exit the library and pull my pack of smokes out of my pocket. I could really use something stronger than this to settle my nerves. Lighting my cigarette, I take the five-minute walk towards her dorm building.

I wonder if she's pissed about my no-show yesterday. I should have sent her a message or something to let her know I couldn't make it. It was a bit difficult when I had to bail my twin out of his latest fucking mess.

The closer I get to her building, the more the dread sets in. I'm not used to this feeling, this need to protect a girl. I'd protect my family, take a bullet for them. But with Livvy, it's different. It's like I want to lock her away in a house guarded by a thousand men, so nothing can get to her. Except she thinks I'm some dumbass, spoiled playboy—especially with that cheerleader continuing to spew those lies.

Livvy doesn't know the real me. I can't let her know the real me. If she did, she'd never want to speak to me again. And I need her. Her lightness seeps into the darkest parts of my soul, igniting a flame inside me that's never been lit before. I never believed in soul mates or past lives prior to Livvy. But now I'm convinced we must have been lovers in some distant time.

When I see two girls exiting the building, I run up the steps. "Hold the door," I yell out to them.

Their eyes widen but they comply. "Sure thing, Romeo. Anything else I can do for you?" a tall blonde asks.

"Nope, thanks." I give them a wink as I pass and take the stairs two at a time. Why the fuck does she have to be on the fourth floor?

By the time I get to her room, my blood is pumping and I'm ramped up from fucking nerves. My fist bangs on the thin wooden door.

"Livvy?" I yell through the barrier. A few students peek their heads out and stare across the hall, but I don't care. I pound my fist down again, in rapid succession. "Livvy, it's me—Romeo. Open up," I call out and knock again.

"Romeo, I'm... not well right now." Her voice is quiet, hoarse. Is she sick?

"Livvy, either open the fucking door or I'll break it down," I tell her.

"I can't. Just go, please," she says, and I hear her footsteps shuffle farther into her dorm room.

I don't need to break the door down. I pull out the small pick from my back pocket. It takes less than a minute to unlock it. Pushing the door open, I close it behind me. The room is pitch-black. "Livvy?" I call more softly this time. My hand slides along the wall, flicking the light on when I find the switch.

"No, turn it off," Livvy rushes out. She's sitting on her bed, against the corner, with her legs folded up under her chin. Her head is down with her hair hanging loose and curtaining her face. Ignoring her request, I slowly approach the bed and take a seat. I bring my hand up to brush her hair away. "No! don't touch me!" she hisses at the top of her lungs. Her head lifts abruptly and her hand swats at mine.

I have never felt so fucking broken before. It takes everything in me not to throw up right now. Raw, primal rage runs through my veins. The need to hunt, to kill, has never been so strong. "Wh... what happened? Who the fuck did this to you?" I ask her, and my voice breaks. It's barely a whisper.

Livvy stares at me, shaking her head. Her face is... it's almost unrecognizable. Her eye's swollen, her lip split open. And there's dried blood in her hair.

"I need to know who did this?" I ask again.

"I don't know... there was two of them." Her body is racked by sobs.

"I'm going to pick you up, Livvy. I'm going to carry you out of here and take you to my place. You need a doctor. I can get a doctor to come to the house," I tell her. I'm not letting her argue with me. I reach over and scoop her up bridal style as carefully as I can. Which isn't easy when she's fighting me.

"No, put me down! Stop, please, no! I can't." She

cries as her fists slam against my body, making contact wherever she can.

Holding her firmly against my chest, I wait. She can hit me as much as she needs to. "Shh, I'm not going to hurt you, Liv. I'd never fucking hurt you," I whisper.

"I just, please, just leave me here," she pleads.

"I can't do that. You need a doctor, Liv. Let me help you." My hand gently brushes over the top of her head. Shifting, I pull my phone out of my pocket and call my brother.

"What's up?" he answers.

"Luc... I..." Shit, I can't even form a sentence—my voice is so fucking choked up.

"Romeo, where are you?"

"I'm at Livvy's place. I... I need you to come and pick us up. Now."

"On my way. I'll be there in five," he says. No questions. No arguments. He knows it's bad. He can tell. I hear the sound of his keys jiggling right before the sound of his engine roaring.

"Hurry," I say, hanging up. "Come on, let's get you out of here." I look around and see a throw blanket on the end of her bed. Picking it up, I drape it over her head. She doesn't need all the nosey bastards in these halls seeing her like this.

Her body calms and her fists clench into my shirt as I push to my feet and carry her out of the building. By the time I make it out back, Luca is pulling into the lot. He opens the door and I climb in, keeping Livvy on

157

my lap. He jumps in the driver's seat and looks back at her, then his eyes meet mine.

"What happened?"

I shake my head. I can't talk. I'm barely holding it together. The rage I have coursing through me right now is unmatched. I've never felt like this.

Luca is calling the doc as we pull into the garage. I carry Livvy up to my room, sit on the bed, lean my back against the headboard, and hold her against my chest. Her quiet sobs are fucking breaking me.

"I'm sorry. I'm so sorry," I whisper into her hair. Her only response is to cry harder. "Tell me what I can do? Livvy, what do you need?" I ask her. I can't just sit here twiddling my fucking thumbs. I need to do something. I need to fix this for her; however, I fear this is the one thing I'm never going to be able to fucking fix.

Livvy shakes her head. There are no words, only more sobs.

"Do you... want me to call your parents?" I ask her. Fuck, maybe I should call my mom, have her come here. I don't know what the fuck happened, the extent of her... attack. And honestly, I can't bring myself to fucking ask. Because without hearing the words, I know. Deep down, I fucking know what happened and the thought makes me fucking sick. Whoever did this, I will make them suffer like they've never imagined. I don't care how long it takes me. I will fucking find them.

"I... can I use your shower?" Livvy asks.

"Of course you can. Come on." I push to my feet with her in my arms. I can't bring myself to let her go. Walking into the bathroom, I turn on the water. And lower Livvy to the floor, catching her when her legs buckle beneath her. "Livvy, when did this happen?" I ask.

"Last—last night," she says.

Fucking hell, she's been alone all this time. This happened last night. I should have been there. My men should have been there. But they weren't.

Because. I. Was. Supposed. To be there.

This is all my fault. I did this to her... How... how did I fuck up so completely? "I should have been there." I say it aloud this time. "I should have been with you. I'm so sorry. I can't... I'm sorry." I don't know what to say.

This is my fault, I remind myself. If I'd been with her, this wouldn't have fucking happened.

"Don't be. It's not your fault," she says, as if reading my thoughts.

"It is. I should have fucking been with you."

She jolts at my harsh tone. Fuck. "I'm sorry. I... let me help you," I tell her, reaching for the hem of her shirt.

Chapter Twenty

Livvy

Romeo reaches for my shirt. My crossed arms hold the fabric against my body.

"No, I can't. I don't want... you can't see me like this, Romeo. Please." I fall to the ground on my knees, hissing as pain radiates through my body. Romeo sits down in front of me and takes my hands in his, holding them still. Firm but not capturing, a grip that tells me he'll let go if I want him to. His eyes focus in on the bruising that wraps around my wrists. I feel his fingers tremble as he inhales a breath.

"Nothing will make me see you any differently, Livvy. Let me help you... please." His voice is quiet. He says that this won't make a difference in how he sees me, but it will.

How could it not? I'm dirty, used, abused. Why would someone like Romeo want anything to do with me now? That isn't even what I should be worried about. Not after everything. I just can't help but think those men took more from me than my choice. They've taken a future I didn't know I wanted.

Romeo lifts my shirt over my head. I can't look at him. I don't want to see the expression of pity in his eyes. I don't want to see the disgust there.

"Come on," he says gently, pulling me up. His fingers grip the waistband of my sweatpants. "Livvy, I will never hurt you. You know that, right?" he reminds me before he pulls the pants down my legs. He curses in Italian. "Fucking dead. They're all fucking dead," he hisses under his breath.

I don't want this. I don't want what happened to me to impact others. I should just leave. Even as I think this, I can't deny that being with Romeo is like being wrapped in a safety blanket.

He steps into the shower fully clothed. I follow him and stand under the warm water. I reach for his body-wash, and the moment the scent fills my nostrils, something calms me. Just a little. Romeo takes the bottle from my hand and squirts some on a loofah; he then proceeds to run the suds over my skin. Laying gentle kisses over some of my bruises. Tears flow freely from my eyes.

"I will never let anything happen to you again. I promise," he says.

That Russian voice comes back into my head. *Next time, I'll make sure it's my turn.* They're going to come back for me. I know they will. "You can't promise that Romeo," I tell him.

"Yes, I fucking can," he grits out between clenched teeth.

I nod my head. I don't want to anger him. I don't want to upset him. If he believes he can protect me, help me, then I'll just let him believe that. I know that he can't always be with me though. Maybe it would be better if I just went home. I could go home and this could all just be over. A bad dream, a nightmare. I can pretend it didn't really happen.

Except... it did happen. And no matter how hard I try to block it from my memory, I can't. Every time I close my eyes, I see them. I can still feel their touch on my skin.

Snatching the loofah from Romeo's hand, I pour more of the soap onto it and viciously scrub at my body. "I can't get it off. I need to get it off," I cry as I continue to scrub harder.

Romeo takes hold of my hands again. "Livvy,

you're okay. You're okay." He wraps his arms around me and holds me tight to his chest.

I shove him off me. "No, I'm not. It's not okay, Romeo. I need to get it off me. Why won't it come off?" I scream.

He takes a step back, lifting his hands in surrender. "I don't know. Fuck, Livvy, I don't know. Tell me what to do."

I shake my head. There isn't anything he can do. Instead of responding, I squeeze more soap on the loofah and wash my skin again.

"Babe, you're going to hurt yourself. Stop." Romeo snatches the loofah from my hands.

"I can't stop. I need to get clean. I need to wash them off me," I tell him.

His face hardens, his jaw clenches. "Livvy, you are clean. Listen to me. It's just you and me here. It's only my hands touching you," he says as he runs his palms up and down my arms. "It's just you and me, Liv."

"Just you," I agree, although I can still feel *them* on me. I try to imagine that it's just Romeo, that I really am alone with him. I don't know if I'll ever be alone again.

"Come on, let's get you dried off." Romeo takes hold of my hand and I let him lead me out of the shower, even though all I want to do is stay under the hot water until I'm clean.

Once I'm dried, Romeo passes me a shirt, one of

163

his, and a pair of his sweatpants. I put the clothes on and sit on the bed. "I'm sorry," I tell him.

He squats down in front of me. "Babe, you have nothing to be sorry about. You haven't done anything wrong.

"I would understand, you know. If you want me to leave, I get it."

"I don't think you do get it, Livvy. You're not fucking leaving. I'm not going anywhere. I'm here, and I'm not going anywhere." He leans forward, and I flinch the moment I see his lips heading for my skin. I hate myself for it. I hate the hurt I see in his eyes when he stops mid-movement. "I'm going to get you something to eat." He stands and heads to the door, before pivoting to face me again. "Do you want me to call anyone, Livvy? Your mom? Sandra?"

I shake my head. "I... I don't want them to know," I tell him with tears rolling down my cheeks. He nods and walks out.

I look around the room. I'm safe here. No one can hurt me here. I don't know why I feel so safe in this room. I don't understand it. But I am going to lean into that feeling right now. I need it. I crawl up the bed and sit with my back against the headboard, bringing my knees up to my chest, and rest my chin on them. I don't know what I'm supposed to do. I just need someone to tell me what to do...

How do I escape this?

When the door opens again, I'm expecting it to be

Romeo. It's not. It's Luca. My eyes search the room for another exit. There isn't one.

"Livvy, Romeo wanted me to bring you this." He places a tray of food on the edge of the bed. "Is there anything I can get you?"

I shake my head. He looks at me for a moment before he turns and walks away. "Luca?" I call out to stop him.

"Yeah?" he asks, turning around.

"Where's Romeo?"

"Ah, he, uh, he had an errand to run. He'll be back soon," he says.

He left me here... alone? He said he wasn't going anywhere. He said he was going to be here with me?

"I can leave." I quickly push off the bed and stand, my arms curling against myself. I feel so small.

"The doctor will be here soon to see you, Livvy," Luca replies.

"I don't need a doctor. I'm just going to go."

He pulls a gun out from behind his back, and I freeze. Again. When my fight or flight instincts should be kicking in, I freeze.

"Do you know how to use one of these?" he asks, holding it out to me. My brows furrow. Why is he giving me a gun?

I nod my head. Yes, I know how to shoot. My dad taught me and my sister.

"Take it. Keep it. If anyone who walks in here

scares you, then shoot 'em." Luca shrugs, like it's no big deal.

I take the handgun, wondering if I really could do it. If I could shoot someone. "Why do you have a gun, Luca?"

"What has Romeo told you about our family?" he questions me instead.

"Nothing. Why?" Romeo really hasn't said anything about his family, and honestly, I've been burying my head in the sand when it comes to the information I've seen online.

"Okay, what have you read about us?"

"A lot, and not much of it good," I admit.

"We're not bad people, Livvy. I promise you you're safe here. At this point, you're practically my sister, which makes you family. And no matter what you read about the Valentinos, we stick together. We protect our own."

Yeah, well, I could have used that protection last night... But I don't say that part out loud.

Chapter Twenty-One

Romeo

I walked out of the house. I had to get out of there. I told Luca not to leave, to make sure she was okay, and then I just drove off. I ended up sitting in some hole-in-the-wall dive bar. I didn't even grab my fucking wallet before I left. That hasn't stopped me from racking up a tab here. The bartender hasn't asked any questions. He just makes sure to refill my glass as soon as it's empty.

I know I need to be stronger. I am fucking stronger than this. She deserves more than this. But I cannot erase the picture of her beaten and bruised body. It took every ounce of patience I had in that shower not to go ballistic. Not to demand information I know she's not ready to give me. I need a description. That's it. Just a description, so I can hunt down the fucking assholes who did this to her.

Picking up the glass, I down it in one gulp, slamming it back down on the bar top. I look at the few patrons around me. Any one of them could be the guy who attacked Livvy. Fuck, I need to get out of here. Standing, I fall straight on my ass. My head spins as the alcohol swirls through my bloodstream. It was supposed to numb me. It hasn't.

I still feel it. All of it. All of her hurt, her despair, her fear. I fucking feel it at my core. In the center of my chest. Like a weight that makes it near impossible to breathe.

"I'll be back tomorrow to pay my tab."

The bartender nods at my slurred words. He must know who I am. Why else would he be letting me walk out without paying?

I stumble onto the sidewalk and start to make my way down the block. When I see two cops at the corner, I glare in their direction. I fucking hate cops.

"Hey, hold up," one of them says to me.

"Why the fuck should I?" I spit back at them,

trying to get my eyes focused enough to read the numbers on their badges.

"We're going to need you to do a sobriety test," the second cop says, a hand resting on his sidearm.

I smirk. I know he's trying to be intimidating. He's not. Not in the slightest. "I'm not driving. Why the fuck do I need a sobriety test?"

"Because I'm the fucking law and I said so," the first fucker replies.

"You're the law, huh? Why don't you get on that little walkie-talkie and tell your captain who you two clowns are fucking with right now—see what he has to say about it?" I suggest.

"And who is that exactly?" The other smart-mouthed cop raises an incredulous brow at me.

Tilting my head, I squint my eyes at him. "Romeo Valentino. I'm sure you've heard of me."

They both laugh. "Yeah, and I'm fucking Mother Theresa. Turn around, hands behind your back. You're under arrest."

"For what?" I scoff, taking a step to the left and stumbling when he reaches for me.

"Drunk and disorderly. Trust me. We're doing you a favor. You think you'll last long out on these streets impersonating a Valentino?"

This has me chuckling for the first time tonight. "I'm not fucking impersonating shit, asshole. I *am* fucking Romeo Valentino."

* * *

I wake with a crick in my neck and pounding in my temples. Opening my eyes, I'm greeted by sunlight and bars. Fucking jail bars.

How the fuck did I end up in here?

The last thing I remember was sitting my ass down at some dive bar.

"Wake up. Your hearing is set to start in thirty minutes," a voice I know all too well says. Captain George.

"Hearing for what?" I ask.

"You were arrested for a drunk and disorderly. Don't worry, the charges aren't going to stick," he says.

"No fucking shit."

* * *

I'd rather spend another night in jail, then sit in the courtroom with Matteo and my father again. I've been given nothing but the silent treatment from Pops. Honestly, I'd prefer the yelling, to have him throw something at me. I climb into the back of the car, after Matteo, and rest my head against the seat. When I close my eyes, all I can see is Livvy. I fucking let her down. Again.

"How was jail?" Matteo asks.

Opening one eye, I give him my best scowl. "I've slept in nicer places."

"You're a fucking trust fund brat. Of course you've slept in nicer places. Care to tell me what made you drink yourself stupid?" He attempts to glare back. It has no effect on me today.

"Not particularly," I tell him, closing my eyes again.

"Well, it's either me or Pops. Or worse, Theo. So come on out with it. I can't help you if you don't tell me what the fuck had you trying to drink your problems away."

"You wouldn't understand," I say.

"Try me."

I roll my eyes. I don't know why I'm going to tell him this. But maybe he can give me some guidance on what to do here. "There's this girl..."

"There's always a girl." He laughs.

"Forget I said anything." I lean my head back and close my eyes again.

"Come on, what about the girl?" he pushes.

"I like her a little too fucking much. That's never happened before." I shrug, like it's no big deal. It is. But he doesn't need to know that.

"You drank yourself stupid, put yourself in a fucking vulnerable position, because you like a girl?" Matteo asks.

"Told you, you wouldn't understand," I grunt.

"Yeah, because I haven't been in love with the same girl since I was fucking six." He's referring to his best friend—the one he's been pining over for years.

"How is Savvy?" I ask, in an attempt to change the subject. I smirk, thinking about the feisty little blonde.

"Nice try. We're not finished. Does this girl have a name?"

"She does, but you're not getting it. I don't need you and Theo running your little checks and shit. She's fucking pure, innocent. Way too fucking good for our family."

"If you like her, then tell her," he says.

"Yeah, that's not going to happen," I tell him, especially after what I've put her through. How I've failed her.

"Why not?"

"Didn't you hear me? She's too fucking innocent for our family."

Matteo's phone starts playing "Best Friend" by Saweetie—that's his ringtone for Savvy. I close my eyes, lean my head back against the seat again, and tune out his conversation. Well, mostly tune it out.

"Heading to my parents' place. Romeo seems to be living up to his namesake and is making stupid fucking decisions in the name of love." Matteo laughs, which has my eyes popping open and my glare aimed at him.

"It's not love," I groan.

"Yeah, well, we all do stupid shit for those we love," Savvy replies. Ignoring their conversation again, I look out the window. We're pulling up to our parents' house. Great, just what I fucking need.

Once we exit the car, I turn to Matteo. "Don't repeat what I told you."

"Sure, but just so you know, I think any girl would be fucking lucky to have you, regardless of what your last name might be," he says with the utmost sincerity. The moment we enter the house, our mom is waiting in the foyer. "Okay, I'm out. I've done my part. This is all you, bro," Matteo says, slapping me on the shoulder.

"Don't you bloody move. You'll be next," Mom points a finger in his direction, and my brother stops moving altogether.

"What'd I do?" he asks.

"Romeo, care to explain why you were out, by yourself. Drunk enough to get arrested?" She folds her arms over her chest. Great, it's angry mom. She's a hot-headed, fiery little woman when she gets mad. Which isn't often.

"I'm in college, Ma. Getting wasted is what college kids do." I shrug.

"Maybe, but you're not like most college kids, Romeo. You can't let your guard down like that. What if..." Mom lets her sentence trail off.

"I'm fine, Ma. Nothing happened." I wrap my arms around her and kiss her cheek.

"But it could have," she whispers.

"I won't do it again," I promise.

"Good. Now, your father wants to see you in his office." She steels her spine.

"Great. Looking forward to it," I say sarcastically as I make my way down the hall.

I knock twice on my father's office door.

"Enter," he calls out from the other side.

I walk in and wait. I know I'm about to get a lecture.

"Sit down." He points to one of the chairs in front of his desk, and I take a seat. "Explain to me why you felt the need to go out and be so fucking reckless last night. Because I'm trying really hard to understand here, Romeo, but I can't for the life of me figure out why you'd do such a thing?"

"I felt like a drink. That's all. I got carried away. I'm sorry. It won't happen again," I tell him.

"You're right. It won't happen again." His gaze searches mine. "Why wasn't Luca with you?"

"Because we're not conjoined. Just your average, everyday twins." I shrug.

"Now is not the time for your smart mouth, Romeo."

I roll my eyes. No shit. I get it. I was reckless. But, fuck, it was one time. People need to loosen up a bit. "Luca had other shit to do."

"I don't want you going out by yourself. Take one of the guys with you next time."

"Sure," I agree. Anything to get me out of here. I need to get home. I need to grovel to Livvy and hope like hell she'll forgive me for leaving her there all night.

Chapter Twenty-Two

Livvy

Romeo never came back. I've been awake all night waiting for him. He didn't show. I don't blame him really. I mean, look at me. I'm a broken mess.

I'm... damaged.

When the doctor stopped by last night, I begged Luca to send him away. Just the thought of someone touching me sent me into a panic. He didn't like doing it, but he did send the doctor home. I didn't see much of Luca after that. Every now and then, he'd pop his head in the doorway to ask if I wanted anything. The answer was always no.

The only thing I want—no, the only *person* I want right now isn't here. I was a fool to think that Romeo could be that person, the one I could lean on. My safety net. I know better than to rely on someone else. I'm an independent woman. I make my own choices.

Except I don't always get to, do I? That has never been more evident than it is right now.

I slide off the bed and stand. I ache. Everywhere. Pushing through the pain, I tiptoe across the bedroom. Maybe I can sneak out of the house without Luca seeing. It will save the humiliation of being kicked out when Romeo does finally return. Opening the door, I realize my attempts at an escape are a no-go when Luca jumps to his feet from where he was sitting just outside the room.

"Do you need something?" he asks.

"Why are you on the floor out here?"

"I... I just wanted to be close, in case you needed something." He shrugs his words off like they're not a big deal. My eyes well up at his kindness. I was wary of Luca when I first met him. Now I'm starting to see behind the tough, playboy exterior he wears like a suit of armor.

"Thank you. But you didn't need to do that."

"Yeah, I did. Come on, I'll get you some breakfast."

176

"I'm not hungry," I tell him, following him into the kitchen. I tried to eat last night. I really did. I just couldn't stomach it.

"Liv, you didn't eat anything yesterday. You need to eat. At least let me make you a smoothie."

"Coffee?" I suggest instead.

"Deal." He smiles as he turns on the coffee machine and grabs two mugs from the cabinets.

I do my best not to wince as I sit on the stool at the breakfast bar. Luca's face tenses. He looks at me and then walks into the pantry, returning with a bottle of aspirin and placing it on the counter in front of me. He doesn't say anything as he fills a glass of water and sets it beside the medication.

"Thank you," I say quietly.

"You know, whoever did this to you, they're not going to get away with it."

"I can't go to the police, Luca. If I do that, my dad will find out. My parents can't know," I plead, my voice desperate. I can hear it.

"I would never leave real justice to the cops, sweetheart. I just mean... we will find them and make sure they can't do this to anyone else."

Then it clicks. What he means. I can't let them do that for me. "I don't want that. I don't want Romeo *or you* to do anything that will ruin your lives because of me."

"That's cute," he says. "Are you really not going to tell your family? You need to tell someone. You need someone to talk to, Livvy." He's quick to change the subject.

"I can't. It's enough that you know. That Romeo knows, and now he's..." I shut my mouth. I will not be *that* girl. I will not sound as pathetic as I feel. If Romeo wanted to be here, like he promised he did, then he would be.

"He *what*?" Luca asks.

"It doesn't matter. I should probably go before he comes back anyway." I open the aspirin bottle, remove two pills, and swallow them with the water.

"Why would you do that?" Luca questions, tilting his head slightly sideways at me.

"It's obvious he doesn't want me here, Luca. I appreciate you trying to spare my feelings but you don't need to pretend," I tell him, doing my best not to tear up.

"I don't know what on earth gave you that idea, but you couldn't be more wrong. If Romeo didn't want you here, he never would have brought you here."

"He left. He didn't come back. People change their minds. It's okay." I stand from my seat. *Wrong move.* Everything hurts with the slightest action.

"Sit down. You're not leaving. Romeo didn't leave because he doesn't want you here. He just needed space, time to clear his head. He hasn't ever felt... well, you bring out a different side of him and he doesn't really know how to deal with it. Seeing you like this, it fucking hurts him Livvy. It's tearing him apart and he's blaming himself for not being with you."

I didn't really consider that this would be hurting Romeo. The only thing I thought of was how disgusted he must be with me now. I don't know him well enough to know how he's feeling. We haven't spoken about feelings all that much. "It's not his fault. He didn't do this to me. Those Russian men did. Romeo can't shoulder the blame for someone else's actions."

Luca spins around, forgetting the coffee he was pouring. "What did you just say?" he asks, his voice suddenly feral. Lethal.

I'm taken aback by his tone. "It's not his fault..." I repeat.

"No, the other bit. Who did this to you, Livvy?"

"I don't know," I tell him, honestly. Because I don't.

"You just said they were Russian. How do you know they were Russian?" he presses.

"They had accents."

"What else? What'd they look like? Old, young?"

I shake my head. I've been trying not to see those two men in my mind. Why is he asking me this?

"What else, Livvy?"

"I don't know. It was dark." I shake my head. "One of them had a scar on his cheek."

As soon as I say the words, it's like a lightbulb goes off in Luca's head. "I'm going to fucking kill him."

"Not before I fucking do." A growly voice comes from behind us, and I jump. Which then has me wincing. "Shit, I'm sorry. I didn't mean to scare you," Romeo says, walking up. My body stiffens when I see him about to lean into me, and he stops. "Have you eaten? Let me get you some breakfast." He walks around the counter and opens the fridge.

"On that note, I'm out. Bro, you stink like a fucking brewery. Go shower." Luca stalks away and I almost want to ask him to stay.

I want that buffer between me and Romeo. I don't know if I'm really ready to face the reality of whatever is going to happen between us. How he's really feeling about everything. The silence is deafening. I want to say something. I just don't know what to say. So, instead, I watch as Romeo retrieves ingredients from the fridge and starts making an omelet, which I'm not going to be able to eat anyway.

Neither of us says a word as he chops up vegetables. It's not until he places a plate in front of me and one next to me that I speak up. "I'm really not that hungry." My voice is low.

"Just try it. Eat a little bit. Please," he says, sitting beside me at the counter. I grab my fork and move it around the omelet, picking at the food. "I'm sorry I left last night. I shouldn't have." Romeo mumbles quietly.

"Where'd you go?" I ask him.

"I, ah, I went to a bar, ended up in lockup overnight."

"You went to jail? Why?"

"Allegedly, I was drunk and disorderly."

180

"Allegedly?"

"I may have had too much to drink," he admits.

"Why?" I ask. I haven't known Romeo that long, but in all that time, I've never heard him talk about college parties or drinking himself stupid.

"Why did I feel the need to drink more than I should have? I don't know, Livvy. My girlfriend was…" He lets the sentence trail off.

"Raped… I was raped, Romeo," I yell the words and jump to my feet. A sudden rage fills me. "You can say it. I'm sorry that I'm no longer the perfect version of me you wanted. I'm sorry I can't live up to whatever fantasy you created in your head. I was raped. I didn't get a choice. I didn't…" My shouts subside, turning into sobs. Romeo's arms wrap around me, and I stiffen.

He doesn't let go though. He just holds me tighter. "I'm sorry," he whispers over and over again. "I will never be able to show you just how fucking sorry I am. I should have been there."

"I… what am I supposed to do now?" I ask him through the tears.

"We will do this together, Livvy. Whatever you need, just say the word and I'll make sure you get it."

"I need it to go away. I need to stop seeing him. I need to make it stop." I cry. I know I'm asking him something no one can give me.

"I fucking wish I could take all of your pain, Liv. I promise you those assholes won't do this to you again. I'll make sure they can't do this to anyone."

I know what he's saying. He's going to go after them. He's going to kill them. "No, I don't want that. I don't want your soul tainted because of me, Romeo. Please, let's just forget about it."

"Babe, I gave up my soul a long time ago. I'm soulless," he says, and I can hear the start of a smirk. "You once asked me if I could kill for love. And, right now, I've never had a better reason to follow through." His lips touch the top of my head.

I push back from him. "No, please. I can't lose you, Romeo. Don't do anything that will get you in trouble. I'm not worth it. They're not worth it."

"Livvy, I wouldn't just kill for you. I'd make the Grim Reaper look like the fucking Tooth Fairy." Romeo has so much conviction in his voice. And I know these are not empty words. They're a promise.

Chapter Twenty-Three

Romeo

I knew the minute Luca walked out of the kitchen that he'd be on the job of finding the assholes who attacked Livvy. As soon as I stumbled in and heard her description of the fuckers, I was ready to stalk right back out and go hunt them down myself.

Then I took one look at her. I fucking left her last night. I knew how hurt she was and I wasn't fucking here for her. It's a wonder she's still speaking to me at this point. It took her hours to stop crying. I picked her up and carried her to the sofa. We haven't moved since. She fell asleep about thirty minutes ago. Her head resting on my chest, her fingers clenched around the fabric of my shirt. I don't want to wake her, so I've sat as still as I possibly can to let her sleep. God only knows how much sleep she had last night. If any...

Luca walks into the living room and looks down at her, concern written all over his face.

"She refused to let Doc see her," he says, sitting in the single sofa opposite me.

"Why didn't you make her? She needs to see a doctor. Call him back." I hiss.

"She was distraught, screaming. She was fucking scared, Romeo. I did whatever I had to do to make her feel safe. You weren't fucking here. You left. I swear to God you need to get your shit together, bro. This isn't about you. It's about her, and right now, she fucking needs you more than she ever will."

"I know that," I grunt.

"Do you? Because I know the only thing you're thinking of right now is going and taking your rage out on a certain Petrov."

"Did you find 'em?"

"Of course I did. But you need to let me or Matteo deal with this. You can't leave her."

"No. I need to do this," I tell him. "She'll understand," I add, not sure if I'm trying to convince him or myself.

"Yeah, that's doubtful. But, for some reason, she loves you and sooner or later you're gonna have to tell her who you are."

"She knows who I am."

"No, she doesn't. She knows what she's read online about our family, which honestly is probably a better picture than the reality."

"I can't lose her," I admit. I'm fucking petrified of losing her and I only just got her.

"Well, if you don't sort your shit out, you're going to," Luca grunts and stands.

"Thank you for staying here last night, for looking out for her."

"Always. What do you want me to do about the two bastards in the warehouse?"

"Keep 'em there. I know I shouldn't leave her, but I have to do it."

"Your call." He shrugs and walks out the door.

* * *

"Please don't leave me." Livvy's pleas tear me apart.

"I'm going to be back before you know it, and my cousin will be here. She's a little unhinged but perfectly capable," I tell her.

Her brows furrow. "Capable of what?"

"Of... anything. Anything I can do. She's family. She's trained in the same shit I've been."

"Which is?"

"Combat. Look, I know there are things we need to talk about. And we will. I promise. But right now, I really do need to go and run an errand." I rake a hand through my hair. I don't want to fucking leave her, but there's a strong part of me that needs vengeance.

"I can go. You don't need to get me a babysitter, Romeo. I'll just go back to my room."

"I want you to stay. I want to know that you'll still be here when I get home. I want you here, Livvy. More than anything." If I have to stay to make sure she does, I will.

"Okay, I'll stay. But I need to know that you're not going to go do something stupid."

"I promise. I won't do anything stupid." I smirk at her. Nothing I do is stupid, and what I'm about to do is the furthest thing from it.

"Romeo, please don't do it. Don't go after them. I just want to forget it all, and I can't do that knowing you've done something immoral."

"Babe." I wrap an arm around her shoulder and pull her into my chest. She's a little rigid, and I'm a gentle as I can be so I don't hurt her. "I won't lie to you. Ever."

"Then don't. Just promise me you're not going to go after them."

"I can't do that," I tell her.

"Some consequences yet hanging in the stars. Shall bitterly begin," Livvy whispers the Shakespearean

186

quote. "Nothing good ever comes from vengeance, Romeo."

"Justice, that's what comes from vengeance." I kiss the top of her head. "I'll be back as soon as I can." With that, I walk out. I introduced her to Izzy when she turned up twenty minutes ago. It's taken me that long to actually manage to leave the bedroom. The guilt that consumes me is unlike anything I've ever felt. I'm tempted to say fuck it and let Luca deal with the assholes for me. What does it really matter if it's me or him who kills them? But I know that it will matter to me. I won't be able to get past it if I don't end them myself.

"How is she?" Izzy asks when I walk through to the foyer.

"Not great," I grunt.

"She will push through this, Romeo. Just go do what you have to do. Don't worry about her. I won't let anything happen," Izzy promises.

"Thank you."

I feel like I've been waiting years for this moment. Blood is pumping through my veins. I can feel the adrenaline. The rush. I need to fuck these two mother-fuckers up. I'd bathe in their fucking blood if I had the time to waste. As much as I'd love to make this slow, I can't. I need to get back to Livvy. I hate that I had to leave her. I hate that she knows what I'm doing and doesn't approve.

Will she look at me differently? Is this what sends her running? I'm not sure. But if she runs, I will fucking chase her. And I'll catch her.

"You know, my Aunt Angelica once tortured a man by cutting his dick off before shoving it down his throat, meaning the fucker died by choking on his own cock." I tell them the legendary story I've heard my father and uncle mention a few times over the years. Neither of the fuckers currently strung up in my warehouse say a word. No doubt they've already heard of Angelica Valentino. My aunt has a reputation for a reason. "As much as I'd love to take this slow, make you both hurt as much as you hurt her, I don't have the time," I say, approaching them as I retrieve a knife from a holster on my belt. They've both been hung up, naked, beaten but even the work-over my brother and the boys already gave them isn't enough. I doubt it will ever be enough. I go to the one with the scar first. "Dmitri Petrov." I know who he is. I also know what I'm about to do is going to start a war between the families.

Ask me if I give two shits? The answer would be no. Not one little fucking bit.

"You fucked with the wrong girl, stronzo." The shine of the blade catches in the overhead lights and something that has never occurred before happens. Doubt. Not doubt that these fuckers deserve to die, because they do. But doubt that Livvy will ever forgive me for following through. She'll have to, though. Or learn to live with it.

Pushing that little voice away, I position the knife at the bastard's cock. This makes him scream. "No, Please. Fuck no," he yells, trying in vain to move. To pivot and prevent me from taking that favored appendage of his.

I look him right in the eye as I take the sharpened edge and slice right through the base, letting the useless piece of meat hit the floor as blood spurts from his body. "You will bleed out like this. Though you deserve so much worse." I spit in his face before I move on to the next guy.

"No, please. It wasn't me. I didn't do it. It was him," he yells, gesturing to the fucker beside him.

Stephan Petrov, cousin of Dmitri. These two are always together. I have no doubt this fucker was the other guy involved in Livvy's attack. "Why?" I ask him, needing to know the answer. Needing to hear it aloud. The fact that it was my fault. Her connection to my family that damned Livvy to her fate. I don't know why I want him to say it. Perhaps I'm a little masochistic.

"Fuck, I don't know. I was following orders," he cries out.

"Luca, grab the pliers." I look over to my brother, who picks up a pair of pliers from the bench. "It's your lucky day, Stephan, because I'm going to let you live," I tell him, and he visibly relaxes. "I want you to spread the fucking message of what happens when you fucking touch something that belongs to me." I turn to Luca and he hands me the instrument. "Hold his tongue out," I instruct my twin. "I said I'd let him live. I didn't say it'd be easy."

Luca grabs Stephan's tongue, and I slice it off. Within seconds, the Russian bastard passes out from the pain. "What the fuck are they teaching these assholes? Because withstanding a bit of torture isn't it." Luca laughs.

"Who the fuck cares. I want him delivered to the hospital, preferably unrecognizable," I tell Luca before walking out of the warehouse. I need to get back to Livvy. As soon as I'm in the car, I text her.

> Me:
>
> I'm on my way home. Are you okay?

> LIVVY:
>
> Depends on your definition of okay.

I don't like her response. It was a stupid fucking question to ask her. Of course she's not fucking okay.

> Me:
>
> I'll be there in ten.

Chapter Twenty-Four

Livvy

It's been three weeks since Romeo picked me up from my dorm room and brought me back to his place. I haven't left his apartment since. Each day, I thought I could do it. Walk outside. Go to class. I crumbled and ended up back in bed. Romeo hasn't left much either. He's gone out a few times when he couldn't *not go*. But, for the most part, he's been right next to me.

I never asked what he did that night with Luca when he left me here with his cousin, Izzy, who I've come to really like. She's been dropping in every couple of days. We've also been messaging each other nonstop. I know I need to ask him about what it is exactly he does for his family. Just not yet. I want to keep my head in the sand a bit longer. I want to stay in this little cocoon he has created for me.

"You got an A on your Poli Sci essay," Romeo says, walking into the bedroom with his laptop open in his hands.

"How? I didn't submit anything." I'm probably going to have to repeat this whole semester. Romeo managed to get me a doctor's note, explaining my absence to the college. That doesn't mean I get a free pass on my assignments though.

"I did it for you." He smiles.

"You did it for me?"

"Is that so hard to believe?" he asks.

"Well, yeah. You came to me for tutoring, remember?" I remind him. I've known for a while now that Romeo did not need tutoring. Why he lied, paid me for sessions, I have no idea.

"Ah, about that... I, ah... well, I'm not even taking English Lit. I kind of just wanted to get to know you." He shrugs.

"That's... creepy and cute at the same time." I smile. I haven't smiled much these last few weeks, but when I do, it's usually at something Romeo or Luca says.

"What are your plans for Christmas? My family's going to Canada. If you want to come, you can. If you want me to stay here with you, I will. What do you want to do?"

Christmas break is in a couple of days. I should have thought about this already. I'm going to have to leave the apartment. I'm going to have to go home. Except I'm not fully recovered yet, and I can't go home to my parents with so much bruising still visible on my face.

"You go with your family for Christmas. I need to go home and see my own family," I lie.

"I don't want to spend one day without you, Livvy. You expect me to go a whole week?"

"You'll survive, trust me. We can text, call. Every day. The time will fly by."

"No, it won't. Every second I'm not with you hurts." When he says things like this, my heart does a little flip. He is more attentive than I can handle at times. I have no doubt that if I asked him to stay with me, he would. I don't want to take him away from his family during the holidays though. I'll figure something out. "You are coming back, aren't you? If you go home, you will come back, right?" Romeo asks.

"Without a doubt," I tell him with a small smile. I may not be planning on going home. I am, however, planning on coming back here.

"Okay, I'll arrange for the jet to fly you home the day before I have to leave for Canada."

"You don't have to do that. I can arrange a flight."

"I know I don't have to. I want to."

"Okay." My brain whirls, trying to come up with a solution for how I'm going to get out of this whole *going home* thing now. Then a lightbulb goes off.

I pull out my phone and message my high school best friend/ex-boyfriend, Kirk. His family has a cabin not far from town. We always laughed about the fact they chose to have a vacation house so close to home. But, right now, I'm praying it's empty over Christmas. I'm also praying that Kirk will help me. We haven't spoken since I left to come to New York.

Me:

I need your help. Is your cabin empty for Christmas?

He responds right away.

KIRK:

What's wrong? And, yes, it is.

Me:

Can I use it?

KIRK:

What's wrong, Olivia?

Shit, what do I say?

Me:

I'll explain when you pick me up from the airport. I'll send you details later. Thank you so much. Also, please don't mention that I'm coming home. My parents can't know.

KIRK:

Are you in trouble?

Me:

No, please just let me explain later.

It's odd that messaging Kirk is a familiar comfort. We used to tell each other everything. All day, every day. I didn't realize how much I missed having that. I know I was never in love with him. It was never like what I feel for Romeo.

Am I in love with Romeo? I'm 99.9% sure that I am. Then there's that 0.1% that isn't certain I'm not using him as a security blanket right now. Maybe the time away from each other will be eye-opening. Maybe it'll do us both good to get some sort of clarification for what's happening between us.

He's been a saint, considering the circumstances. I don't know too many college guys who would stick around and help someone after what happened to me. I still tense when he tries to hug me or kiss my head. I'm thankful he hasn't tried to do anything more than that.

We haven't kissed; we haven't fooled around at all. Honestly, I know I'm not ready for that. But how long is Romeo prepared to wait?

* * *

As soon as I exit the plane, I find Kirk waiting for me by his car. I'm wearing a huge pair of sunglasses and a black baseball cap, both of which Izzy brought over for me yesterday, along with a suitcase full of clothes. I haven't gone back to my dorm. Romeo offered to go and get my stuff, but I told him to leave it there.

I lied to Sandra, telling her I went home early. I couldn't face her. I don't want to face anyone after what happened to me. It's easier if people don't know.

"Livvy? You need to start explaining some things," Kirk says as he approaches me.

I stop with a hand held out. "Sorry, I will. Let's just get out of here," I say, walking around him and jumping into the passenger seat of his car. My anxiety about being here, being alone with someone, being away from Romeo, is at an all-time high right now. My knee bounces uncontrollably as Kirk starts the engine.

He looks over to me. "What happened?"

"I... I was..." I can't even say the words.

"Shit, Liv. Why didn't you call me?" he asks. "I would have come to New York."

"I don't... I... I just want to forget it, Kirk. My parents can't know about this."

"Where do they think you are?"

"I told them I was going away with my roommate and her family to Vancouver."

"And they were okay with that?" he asks, his eyebrows raising with the question.

"Not at all. But I can't let them see me like this," I say, pulling the glasses off.

"Shit. Olivia, you should have called me," he hisses, with his wide eyes glued to my face.

"Eyes on the road, Kirk."

He shifts his gaze out the windshield again. "So the private jet?" he asks. Although it's not an actual question, I know what he's getting at.

"It's, uh, my boyfriend's. Well, his family's." My voice is quiet, shy almost. I don't think I've uttered those words out loud to anyone. Romeo Valentino is my boyfriend...

"Your boyfriend? Is he... did he do this, Livvy?"

"No, of course not." I scowl at him.

"So, does this boyfriend have a name?"

"Romeo," I say with a smile.

"Of course it is." Kirk laughs.

* * *

Walking through this cabin brings back a lot of good childhood memories. There's a sense of comfort here, safety, but it's missing something.

Not something. Someone. Romeo.

I shake off the sadness. It's only been a few hours. I refuse to believe that I've become that attached to him in such a short amount of time. In all of the years I dated Kirk, I never missed him. Not even during the past six months. I think I missed having that one friend who knows everything about you and never judges. The way I miss Romeo right now is different from that. It's too much. How am I supposed to last a whole week if I can't even last a few hours?

My phone pings in my hand. I turn it over to see the screen, and a smile spreads across my face. It's Romeo. Then panic sets in. He's video-calling me. Shit, I can't answer him yet. I need to get my story straight. Rejecting the call, I send him a message instead.

Me:

I'll call back in a few.

ROMEO:

Is everything okay?

Me:

Yes, fine. Just talking to my parents.

ROMEO:

I miss you already. You know I can ditch my family and come to Covington.

Me:

My dad will shoot you.

ROMEO:

I'll bring Doc with me so he can patch me up afterwards.

ME:

You have an answer for everything.

"So, Romeo, huh? It's serious?" Kirk asks.

I peer up to see him staring at me. "Yeah, I think it is." I smile.

"In all the years I've known you, I've never seen that look on your face," he says.

"What look?"

"Love."

"Kirk, I'm sorry."

"Don't be. We were convenient, Livvy. We both knew we weren't end goals." He shrugs and heads to the kitchen. "I've stocked the fridge and pantry for you, but if you need anything else, just call.

"Thank you. For everything."

"No worries. I'm going to head out. Just, ah, make sure you call if you need anything," he says again.

I nod my head and pray that he doesn't move in for a hug. Thankfully, he reads my body language perfectly and doesn't approach me, exiting the cabin with a wave of his hand instead.

Chapter Twenty-Five

Romeo

Being away from Livvy this past week has been absolute hell. I've thought about getting on a flight to Covington so many times. The one thing that held me back was *her*. She insisted I stay with my family. I just have to hold out two more days. Two more days and she'll be back in New York. Back in my arms. Although, with the shitshow I've returned to, I think she might be better off staying away longer.

I flew back on Boxing Day with Luca and Matteo. We're holed up in Theo's apartment. He went off on some rampage and shot some people he wasn't supposed to. Not that we have a list of people we *are* supposed to take out. Currently... But there are definitely those who we should avoid. He now has three of the five families after him. I don't blame him, though. I would have done the same thing. I *have* done the same thing. The difference is the only witness I left... well, last I heard he was still in a coma and is missing a tongue. He won't be talking to anyone anytime soon.

The assholes my brother took down deserved it. They were planning to auction off his girlfriend—though it's still unclear if she would call herself that—to the highest bidder. Talk about a Christmas full of surprises. And as if all that wasn't enough, turns out Matteo went and got hitched to his best friend Savvy in Vegas, while Theo is dead set on this Maddie chick, who he's attempting to move into his apartment along with her little sister, Lilah.

If we had cameras following us around, I think we'd put the Kardashians to shame in the family drama category of life. The reason we're here is to help protect Theo from himself and the other families who all want his head. Which was a great idea in theory, if he hadn't gone off on his own and got himself fucking shot. He did, apparently, put an end to the rising mafia war. Although, we now have to face why the Russians attacked him in the first place.

"You know, we should just tell them. It's not like Pops doesn't already know," Luca says. He's adamant about wanting to tell Pops and our older brothers about Livvy and the two Russians who ended up in our warehouse.

"If I wanted everyone to know my business, I'd send a fucking memo, Luca."

"It's your call. You know I'll follow you right to hell and back. But, I'm just sayin', this whole Russian feud could be because of us."

"It's not," I deny, even though chances are it is.

"Your call, bro," he says again before asking, "How is Liv doing?"

"She seems fine." I shrug. "You do know you can't go through with donating that kidney." I overheard Theo and Maddie talking about Lilah. Apparently Maddie's little sister is sick and in desperate need of a transplant. We all had to get tested to see if we were matches. Somehow, Luca turned out to be a better match than I did—something about my white blood cell levels being too high or some shit.

"Why the fuck wouldn't I?" he spits.

"What about football? You're in the middle of a season. You really going to step out?"

"Yes."

"You don't even know her, Luca."

"You know, I didn't really know Livvy either before you had me help you kill off a Petrov," he counters. And my fist swings out so quickly. The mention of

Livvy's name has me raging. I'm messed up when it comes to her. Luca swings back, just as hard and fast. Before I know it, we're going at each other blow for blow.

"Matteo! Get your ass out here now!" Theo's voice yells out, right before I'm tugged rearwards by my shirt. I push to my feet and shrug him off, ready to go another round with my twin. "Who the fuck made her cry?" Theo growls, pointing at Lilah. That's when I notice we have an audience. Maddie is standing off to the side with her sister, who's now sobbing into her hands.

"What's going on?" Matteo asks, walking out like he doesn't have a care in the world. Which he probably doesn't. His life is fucking peachy keen right now. He just married the girl of his dreams.

"Where were you while these two fucking heathens were destroying my fucking living room?" Theo yells at him. "And I'm still waiting for an answer from you." He points at me, then Luca.

"Uh, Theo, I'm fine. Really, it wasn't them," Lilah says.

"Then why are you crying?" he asks her.

"Um, I may have overheard Luca tell Romeo about the kidney thing... that he's going to give me a kidney," she says in the quietest voice.

Theo turns back to me. "My office, now!" he yells before shoving me out of the room.

I follow Luca into Theo's office, where we wait for what seems like an eternity before he finally graces us with his presence. Followed by Pops. Fuck. This isn't fucking good.

"Pops, I didn't know you were coming in today," Luca says.

"Clearly," he replies. Heading over to the wet bar, our dad pours himself a drink. "Care to explain why your brother's home looks like a hurricane ran through it?"

I look to Luca. *Don't say a fucking word.* My glare says what I don't. "We just had a minor disagreement. It's nothing. Water under the bridge," I grit out between clenched teeth.

"You're brothers. You're on the same fucking team. We have enough people trying to kill us without killing each other. Whatever this is, sort it out. And whatever Theo has to replace out there." He points in the direction of the living room. "...it's coming out of your allowances."

Fucking hell, Theo's shit is expensive. The fucker likes to show off. Replacing his crap is going to cost a small fortune.

"What? Pops, that's not fair." Luca scowls.

"What's not fair is that your brother took a beating and a fucking bullet for your asses and then you come here and destroy his home."

I look to my older brother. Fuck, did he really get shot because of me? I feel like I might actually throw up. The last thing I want is for anything I do to come back onto my family.

"What are you talking about? What do they have to do with the Russians who jumped me?" Theo questions casually, leaning against the bookshelf. A little too casually if you asked me. The look in his eye, combined with the tick in his jaw, tells me he would love nothing more than to strangle us both.

"That's what I'm here to find out," Pops says, taking a seat on one of the sofas. "Start talking," he directs this at me and Luca.

Matteo curses under his breath and moves across the room, positioning himself next to Theo. And I know it's is show of loyalty. Though I'm also kinda hoping he'll act as a buffer if our brother actually *does* try to kill us.

"It wasn't our fault." Luca is the first to talk.

"It never fucking is," Theo grunts.

"He fucking deserved it. He hurt her in the worst way, so we put him in the hospital," I blurt out.

"Who did you put in the hospital and who did they hurt?" Pops asks. I can tell his patience with us is waning.

"Livvy... That fucker attacked her. He...." I trail off. I can't even say the fucking word. *Rape.* She was fucking raped by those bastards. The fact I let one live is a testament to my own patience. I don't plan on letting him live indefinitely, just long enough to get my message across to the whole fucking city. No one puts a hand on my girl.

"He hurt her, so we hurt him. Stephan Petrov. He

deserved it, Pops, swear it," Luca says. Small truths help cover the omissions. I doubt anyone knows about Dmitri yet, and they won't if I have my way.

"Who is this Livvy?" Pops asks me, ignoring my twin.

"She's, ah, my tutor," I stumble over the truth this time.

"Romeo, you're trying my last nerve here, son. You have a fucking 4.0 GPA. Why the fuck do you need a tutor?" Pops is rubbing at his temples now, which is never a good sign.

"I... I'm not sure. But she is, and I wasn't going to stand by and let that fucker get away with hurting her," I hiss.

"Right," Pops says.

"It's fine, Pops. What's the plan from here?" Theo's words are unexpected. I frown at him. He got shot, beaten down, because Luca and I attacked the Russian bastards and he's saying it's fine. I should question his sanity. I'm not going to though.

"It's done. Eye for an eye and all that bullshit. We hospitalized one of theirs; they put a bullet through one of ours," Pops says. "The Petrovs know nothing about those girls. And we need to fucking keep it that way." He's referring to Maddie and Lilah, who are half Russian and half Italian, and their Russian side just happens to come from the fucking Petrovs.

"Agreed," all four of us say in unison.

"Romeo, we're going for a drive." Pops turns to me.

I swallow. You know you're in deep shit when Pops gets you alone. Don't get me wrong, he'll give you shit all day in front of everyone. But when he pulls you aside for a little one-on-one, you might as well dig your own grave.

I follow him down to the car and climb into the passenger seat.

"You know, I always thought you were the smart one out of all four of my children," Pops says, breaking the tension-thick silence.

Okay, so we're going for the good ol' Italian guilt. Got it.

"I am." I shrug.

"Really, because going after the fucking Petrovs alone wasn't a fucking smart move."

"I know," I admit.

"I'm disappointed. I really thought you boys knew you could come to me with anything, that you could count on me to always have your backs. Why didn't you come to me?" he asks, never taking his eyes off the road.

"I know I can come to you, Pops. This was just something I had to do."

"Do you know how I knew your mother was the one, without a shadow of a doubt?"

"How?"

"When my father was killed, I—well, I didn't handle it the best way. And your mom, she saw me. Really saw me. Saw what I was capable of. She didn't run. She didn't look at me like I was a monster. She accepted me. In my darkest moments, she was the only thing that could give me light."

"I think I get it." I sigh. It's not until we pull up at the private airstrip that I turn and look at him, questioningly. "Why are we here?"

"You have a flight to catch. Go get Olivia and bring her home," he says, handing me a manila folder.

It doesn't surprise me that he knows who Livvy is. Nothing ever gets past my father. The fact that he's handing me *this*, though, that's odd. "What's in the folder?" I ask, almost too afraid to open it.

"The address where you'll find her. She's not at her parents' house, Romeo."

No, that can't be true. She told me she was with her family. Why would she lie to me?

"Just go get her. Bring her home. Romeo... What happened to her, it's going to take a long time for her to heal. If you truly care about this girl, you're going to have to keep that in mind," he says as if he can hear my unspoken thoughts.

"Got it. Thanks, Pops."

"And, next time, fucking come to me first," he grunts as I exit the car.

Chapter Twenty-Six

Livvy

I'm supposed to be returning to New York tomorrow. I'm not really sure I can do it. I want to. I want my life back. I want to be with Romeo. I'm just not one hundred percent sure I can handle the fear of being back in the city. I just keep hearing those words over and over.

Next time, I'll make sure it's my turn.

I swallow another gulp of the vodka I found in the

back of the pantry earlier today. It's been a really long, lonely week. My thoughts have not been healthy. I know that. I've tried to keep myself occupied, tried to remind myself that I won't feel like this forever. At least I hope I won't. It's a lot harder to pretend that you're okay when you're alone and no one is scrutinizing your every move. Those weeks I spent in Romeo's apartment, I could pretend a little. Even when I couldn't, when I felt like there was no hope, he was there to hold me. He let me cry as much as I needed to. When I'd wake up screaming in the middle of the night, he'd be right there, whispering the sweetest promises.

Promises that I was safe. Promises that he was never leaving. Promises that we were going to get past this together.

I wish I'd just gone with him to Canada. Why did I think having space would be a good thing? It hasn't been. I can't say I've been completely alone. Kirk's been dropping in daily to check on me. He never stays long, but it's nice that he stops by. I can at least look at myself in the mirror again now and not see the physical reminders of that night. I wish the internal scars would heal as easily as the bruises.

I jump up when there's a knock at the door. Kirk doesn't usually knock. That knock is also harder and louder than what Kirk would use. My first thought is that they've found me. Who else could it be? I'm in the middle of nowhere.

"Livvy, open the fucking door now," a gravelly voice yells from outside. A voice I know all too well.

I run—okay, maybe stumble a little—to the door and swing it open. And standing on the other side is Romeo.

My Romeo. A not-so-happy Romeo. I don't really care though. I'm so happy to see him, so excited that he's here, that I ignore his scowl and throw my arms around him. He catches me, stopping me from falling on my ass when I trip over the doorstep in my haste to get to him.

"Fuck," he curses, picking me up, walking inside, and kicking the door closed behind him.

My arms cling to his neck as tight as I can, too scared that if I let him go, he'll disappear. "If I'm dreaming, I never want to wake up," I whisper.

Romeo's grip tightens around my waist. "Babe, you're not dreaming. Also, if you ever don't wake up, I will find a voodoo witch to bring you back. I'm not fucking doing this life without you, Livvy."

"Aw, you always say the sweetest things." I giggle, leaning back a little so I can look at his face. Those dark eyes pierce into mine.

"How much have you had to drink? And where the fuck are we, Livvy? Because I'm pretty sure this crappy little cabin isn't your family home."

Oh shit. Romeo is here. In Covington. In Kirk's cabin. "Ah, this is a friend's cabin," I say, untangling myself from him. I sit back on the sofa and pick up the now half-empty bottle of vodka from the coffee table.

Romeo comes over and snatches it out of my hands. "Olivia, why are you here?"

"Oh, it's Olivia now? That means I'm in trouble. Am I in trouble, Romeo?" I ask him.

"That depends on the answer. Why are you here, Livvy?" he asks again, sitting down next to me.

"I couldn't go home," I admit.

"Why not? Did your parents say something? Do something?"

"No, they don't know I'm here. I told them I was spending the holidays with Sandra."

"Okay, why didn't you tell me? I would have taken you with me. Have you been here alone all fucking week?" he asks, looking around the small cabin.

"I didn't want to intrude on your family's Christmas, Romeo, and I like it here." I try to see the cramped living space through his eyes. I can't though. All I see is a lifetime of memories.

The door opens, and within seconds, Romeo is on his feet. I don't see the gun he whips out until Kirk drops the bag of groceries he was holding.

"Shit, Romeo. No. Stop," I say, jumping up and rushing to get in front of him.

"Livvy, move," he says. His voice is feral, a tone I've never heard from him before. I should be scared, but I know he won't hurt me.

"No. Put the gun down. He's my friend."

212

Romeo tilts his head to the side, staring at Kirk and ignoring me completely. "You have five seconds to tell me who the fuck you are and why you're here, with my girlfriend, before I blow your fucking head off."

I gasp. "No!" I yell, my voice firmer. This has Romeo finally turning to me.

"I know you're not cheating on me, Livvy, so why is another man helping himself to the cabin you've been shacked up in."

He knows I'm not cheating on him? I don't know if he's just extra cocky, or really secure in our relationship. Or maybe it's what happened to me that solidifies his certainty.

"It's his cabin, Romeo. This is Kirk, my friend from school. Please just put the damn gun away. You're scaring me," I beg him.

His face pales a little and he lowers the gun. He doesn't put it away. He does, however, wrap one arm around my shoulder and pull me against his body. "I'm sorry. I didn't mean to scare you." He kisses the top of my head, and I sink into him.

"Please don't hurt him. Romeo. He's just my friend. I swear," I plead. I know that Romeo is capable of things I don't even want to consider. He's just showed me a side of him I've never had to see before. A side of him that should have me running for the hills. Instead, here I am, taking comfort in his embrace.

"A friend you used to fucking date," he grunts.

"I promise nothing like that is happening here. He just drops in to bring me food. That's all."

"You should have told me. If I knew you were here alone, I would have come sooner."

"I know you would have," I say, slipping out of his embrace. "So, Romeo, meet Kirk. Kirk, this is Romeo." I point between them.

Kirk is still pale. He nods his head, but doesn't say anything.

"Ah, hey," Romeo says.

"Okay, well, now that we all know each other, I'm going back to my drinking," I announce.

"I dropped the bottle. Sorry, babe." Romeo side-steps me.

"No, you didn't," I counter at the same time Romeo snatches the bottle, walks into the kitchen, and tips the contents down the sink. "Wait! I was enjoying that."

"Yeah, I could tell," he groans.

"Come on, Romeo, it's not like you never drink."

"You're right, which is why I know you'll be thanking me tomorrow when you don't wake up feeling like death," he says as he fills a glass with water. "Drink this instead." He holds the water out in front of me.

"No," I tell him with my arms folded over my chest.

Romeo raises an eyebrow at me. "Please," he adds, the corner of his lips tipping up slightly.

"Stop being charming."

"My name's Romeo. It's hard not to be, babe."

"Shut up." I take the glass and drink the entire thing, slamming it down on the counter when I'm done. "Happy?"

"With you? More than you'll ever know."

"Ah, Livvy, I'm going to just head out if you're all good here," Kirk interjects.

"Yep, I'm good. Thanks, Kirk." I offer him an *I'm sorry* smile. And before he leaves, Kirk lifts his pinky to his right ear. A sign we haven't used in a really long time. It's what we used to do at school to check in with each other. If either of us didn't return the gesture, it meant we weren't fine. Far from it. Lifting my pinkie, I copy the gesture and he relaxes.

"Okay, I'll catch you later." Kirk leaves without acknowledging Romeo.

"I don't like him," Romeo says.

"You don't like anyone," I tell him.

"That's not true. I like you a whole fucking lot. And Luca, I like him."

"One, he's your brother, so he doesn't count. And two, I kind of like you a whole lot too." I smile.

Chapter Twenty-Seven

Romeo

L ivvy is sleeping with her head resting in my lap and her legs stretched out on the sofa. We landed in New York late last night, and I brought her straight back to my place. Where she belongs. I'm fucking fuming that she was alone all week. In that cabin. In the middle of fucking nowhere. And how the fuck did I not know? I should have fucking known.

I'm painfully aware I haven't done this whole boyfriend thing before. I didn't think I'd be so fucking bad at it though. I want to be better. I need to be better. Livvy deserves the best. And right now, I'm not giving her that.

I make a vow to do better.

She stirs, little cries escaping her lips as she sleeps. She's had no one to comfort her during the nightmares. All fucking week. I wonder how much she's been sleeping.

Picking her up, I walk into the bedroom and tuck her under the blankets. I then strip down to my boxers and climb in next to her. As I lie here, watching her sleep, I can see our whole future. I see her as my wife, the mother of our children. I wonder if I can take a page out of Matteo's book and run off to Vegas and get hitched. As much as I'd be okay with that idea, I don't want to rob Livvy of whatever her dream wedding is. As long as I'm the one waiting at the other end of the aisle, I don't care where or how we get married. The result will be the same. Livvy will be a Valentino.

Her eyes open and she looks around frantically.

"Livvy, it's okay. You're safe. You're home." I pull her onto my chest, and my hands smooth out her hair.

"I really missed you, Romeo," she whispers.

"It's a truth universally acknowledged, that a single man in possession of a good fortune, must be in want of a wife," I say, quoting the same Jane Austen phrase we once argued over.

"I guess it's a good thing you're not a single man then, Mr. Valentino." She smiles up at me.

"Marry me," I blurt out.

"What?"

"I want you to always be mine. I want to wake up with you every day. I want to be everything you want and deserve. I don't ever want to be apart from you again, Livvy."

"Romeo, we're nineteen. We can't get married."

"Technically, we can."

"We're nineteen," she repeats.

"I'm aware."

"I think my dad really will shoot you." She grins.

"I can take it," I tell her. "So, is that a yes?"

"Yes."

My eyes widen. She said yes... "I love you so fucking much." I slam my lips down on hers. The moment they touch, I freeze, fully expecting her to pull away. She doesn't though. She leans into me, and her tongue swipes over the seam of my mouth, seeking entrance. I open for her and immediately take over the kiss. Slowly pulling away, I look into her eyes for any sign of anxiety, hurt, anything that will tell me she's not handling this kind of physical affection.

"I'm okay," she assures me.

"It's okay if you're not, you know. I will wait a lifetime just to kiss you, Livvy. If you're never ready for this, that's okay too."

"You'd really marry me knowing you'd never get

laid again? I know how much you like sex, Romeo. I've done it with you, remember?"

"Oh, I remember, fondly. But it's you I love. Everything else is secondary."

"I love you. I'm sorry I'm not my best self right now, but I will work on getting better."

"You don't need to work on anything. You are perfect just the way you are." I lean in, fusing my lips with hers again. Now that I know she's okay with this, I'm not going to stop kissing her until she tells me to. Or until I have to get up and shoot whoever is currently knocking on my fucking door. "Go away."

"Moving truck's here, Romeo. Get your ass up. I'm not your secretary," Luca yells out through the door.

"Moving truck? Are you moving?" Livvy questions me.

"Nope." Standing, I pull my jeans back on, attempting to discreetly hide my boner as I go.

"You know you don't need to hide it. I've seen it." She laughs.

"I don't want to make you uncomfortable," I tell her.

"You're not."

"Be right back." I kiss her forehead and walk out to see the moving guys carrying in boxes. "You can leave it all out here," I tell them, pointing to the living room.

"Ah, what? Why can't they just take it all to your room?" Luca interjects.

"Because Livvy is in there, and I'm not having random men walk in on her when she's in bed, idiot."

He nods in understanding. "Right. How is she?"

"She's... better," I tell him. She's a little better, but she has a very long way to go.

My phone rings from the bedroom and Livvy calls out, "Romeo, it's for you."

I walk back into the room to find her holding my phone, her hand shaking as she stares at the screen. "What's wrong?" I ask, snatching the device from her fingers.

I see a missed call and a message notification, which can be read on the home screen.

SAMANTHA JUNE:

Had a great time last week. Let's do it again soon. xx

"Livvy, this isn't what you think. I don't fucking know who this chick is," I tell her.

"I do," she says.

"What?"

"I know who she is. She's the cheerleader we saw in the cafeteria. The one who seems to think you and her have something going on."

"How do you know it's the same girl?"

"Sandra told me her name was Samantha June." Livvy shrugs.

"Look, she's obviously nuts. I haven't touched the girl. Ever. I promise you that."

"Okay."

"Okay?"

"I trust you, Romeo. If you say there's nothing going on, then I believe you."

"How the fuck did I get so lucky to have you?" I'm not going to lie. I was about to drop to my knees and beg her to believe me. I had every expectation of her getting up and walking out. It would be understandable. It's what most girls would do after reading a message like that. Livvy isn't most girls, though, and that's never been more evident.

"You studied for classes you weren't even taking." She laughs.

"Worth every hour," I tell her. "Come on, I have to show you something." Holding her hand, I lead her out to the living room, which is now piled up with boxes of what little belongings she had in her dorm.

"What is this?" she asks.

"It's all your stuff. You're moving in." I smile, hoping I'm not coming off as crazy as I sound in my own head.

"Wait. You didn't discuss this with her first?" Luca chimes in. "Fuck, Livvy, say the word and I'll have his ass committed to the psych ward. Actually, just blink three times and twitch your nose twice if you need an escape," he adds.

"I... wait, do they have rooms for two in that ward? That could be a fun vacation," she asks, her neck craned in thought.

"Yeah, you two can sort yourselves out. I think you're both equally nuts." Luca leaves the room, shaking his head. And Livvy stares at the boxes silently. For way too long.

"Say something," I beg her.

"You probably should have asked me if I wanted to move in with you, Romeo."

"I didn't know if you'd say yes."

"Well, yeah, that's how questions work."

"I just... I really want to start *us*. Our lives. I want this to be your place just as much as it's mine. I want this to be our place."

"What about Luca?" she asks.

"What about him?"

"What does he think about me living here?"

"He loves the idea," I tell her.

"This is a lot, and fast, Romeo. What happens if, in two weeks' time, you change your mind?"

"That's not going to happen."

"You can't know that."

"I know that I've never had a reason to be a better person. I've never had such a strong reason to wake up every morning and fight for what's mine. Fight for us. I know that I've never loved anyone, anything, like I do you, Livvy."

"I don't know what to say. What if I don't want to live with you yet?"

Well, fuck, the words *too fucking bad* are on the tip of my tongue. But I can't say that to her. As much as I want to force the subject of her living with me, I get that *right now* having a choice is imperative to her. "Then I'll buy you an apartment in this building and you can live there," I offer, instead of the whole *I'll just chain you to my bed* image I have in my head.

Livvy's mouth gapes open. "That's... insane and not happening." She laughs.

"I'm not trying to take away your choice. I should have spoken to you about this first. I didn't think past my need to have you close to me. I'm sorry, and I totally understand if you're not ready for this. I won't like it, but I will do whatever you want to do, babe."

"I'm scared," she says.

"Of what?"

"Of us. I already need you more than I should, Romeo. The week I just spent without you was hell. I hated it. It's not healthy to need someone like that."

"We can be sick together then, because I need you just as much, Liv. This is new to me, and I'm likely to fuck up. A lot. But one thing that won't waver is how much I want you. How much I need you. How much I love you."

Chapter Twenty-Eight

Livvy

I'm either just as crazy as he is. Or worse, *crazier*.

Because, right now, I can't really think of a good reason I shouldn't move in with Romeo. Apart from the obvious ones: we're nineteen and we've really only just met. My parents really are going to want him dead when they find out. All of which I'm choosing to ignore because this man... This gorgeous, beautiful man wants me. '

"*She hardly knew how to suppose that she could be an object of admiration to so great a man.*" Never has a literary quote had so much meaning to me before. Jane Austen really did know what she was talking about.

"Romeo, take me back to bed." My heart hammers in my chest with what I'm about to do. I need to do this. I need to try to take back what they took from me.

"What's wrong? Are you okay?" He grabs my hand in his and starts walking towards his room. Our room?

"I want you to make love to me," I say and his steps stop.

His head turns to look at me. "No, you don't have to do this. We have plenty of time. We can wait."

"I want to do this. I want you to take it away. I want this." I'm more adamant in my decision.

Without saying anything, Romeo continues to escort me into the bedroom, kicking the door shut behind him. He stands at the foot of his bed, his hands trembling as they reach for the hem of the shirt I'm wearing. "If at any point you want to stop, just say the word," he tells me.

I love him for verbalizing it but I already know that he'd stop if I needed him to. Romeo isn't *him*. He isn't the man who forced himself on me. He isn't the one who took away my choice.

"I won't. I love you, Romeo. I want this. I want you," I repeat, because I honestly do. I want him more than anything and I'm praying like hell that I can actually go through with this. That I can get out of my own head long enough to enjoy it.

Reaching for my panties, Romeo slowly drags them down my legs, lifting each foot one at a time and helping me step out of them before guiding me onto the bed. I watch his every move, my nerves rattling as he strips his own clothes off. He lies next to me on the bed, the tips of his fingers trailing up my stomach and circling one nipple before moving on to the next. "You are truly the most exquisite thing I've ever seen," he says, his voice soft, reverent almost.

"Ditto." I smile at him.

Romeo leans in, kissing me softly. His lips run down the length of my neck, before moving lower and wrapping around a nipple. He licks the tip and sucks lightly. My back arches off the bed, as his fingers continue to roam around my stomach. Up my side. So soft. Featherlight.

"Oh..." Pleasure fills me, and I let myself get lost in it.

Romeo refocuses his attention on my other breast, the weight of his body shifting slightly on top of me. I freeze for a second and his head pops up, his eyes connecting with mine. "You good?" he asks.

"Yes, don't stop."

He hesitates for a moment before resuming what he was doing. Lavishing my breasts with attention. His hand travels lower, then starts running up and down my inner thigh, switching from leg to leg. The strokes of his fingers moving higher each time, closer to my core. When they finally connect with my clit, I jolt, and once again Romeo stops. His gaze searching mine. Taking hold of his hand, I place it back on my pussy.

"Don't stop," I tell him.

His fingers start circling my clit and his mouth goes back to my breast. But his eyes... They stay on mine. I let myself float away with the sensation, and before long, I'm flying off that blissful edge. My whole body spasms. When I come back, I'm met by Romeo's cocky smirk. "I've fucking missed seeing that," he says.

"How about you try to make it happen again then? If you think you can," I challenge him.

"Think? Babe, I know I can." He reaches into the bedside drawer and retrieves a condom.

"Romeo, do you think...? Can we..." I don't know how to ask him. I don't want him to use a condom. I want his skin on me. In me. I want him. All of him. But what if he says no? I've been given the all-clear from the doctor Romeo insisted I see a few days after he found me. Thankfully, I've been on birth control since I was sixteen, which was one less thing to be concerned about.

"What?"

"Never mind," I say, rather than tell him what I want.

"Babe, just ask me. What do you need."

"I need you. Can we not use that?" I ask, pointing to the foil wrapper.

Romeo's expression is hard to read. Blank. "Of course. But just know I'm an overachiever, babe. If my swimmers impregnate you, I'm not waiting until graduation to get married." His smirk widens.

"My birth control is rock-solid." I smile.

Dropping the foil packet on the bed, Romeo positions his body on top of me, between my legs. My heart is jumping out of my chest.

I want this. I want this. I want this. I repeat it over and over in my head.

"Remember there is no rush, Livvy. If you want to wait, we can wait. We *will* wait." Romeo holds my face in the palms of his hands.

"I want this. Just... go slow," I tell him.

"Okay."

I feel him position himself at my entrance, and he slowly slides inside me. Pausing when he's fully seated. My body tenses and I close my eyes. I can't help the tears that fall. My mind drifts back to that night and all I can see is *them.* I can feel the damp coldness of the grass beneath me... that bite of pain... the scar...

"Livvy, open your eyes. Look at me," Romeo says. "Look at me. It's me, just us. You and me."

My eyes snap open and I gaze into his. I feel so much love from him. Inhaling deeply, I try to bring myself back to this moment. I'm with Romeo. I'm with the man I love.

"Let's try this." He rolls over, taking me with him

without losing the connection we have. "I want you to go at your own pace. There is no rush, Livvy."

Once I'm on top, looking down at him, I relax, the different position giving me something I didn't know I needed. Control.

I lean over and my lips meet his. "Thank you," I whisper between kisses.

"For what?" he asks.

"For being perfect," I tell him. My hips start to move in small, circular motions. As I sit upright, I feel him deep inside me. The tip of his cock hitting that magic spot with each movement. My hands feel their way over the ridges and grooves of his abs. His pecs. Exploring the contours of a well-formed body. I pick up the pace slightly, my head tips back, and I close my eyes on a moan.

"Fuck, babe, you feel so fucking good riding my cock. Ride me like you stole me, Livvy, because you fucking have. You've stolen every piece of me."

My head straightens and my eyes open in shock. I shouldn't be surprised. The few times we've done this before, Romeo had the filthiest of mouths. He takes his dirty talk to the next level. I can feel myself getting wetter, my walls clenching at his words. It seems I love his filthy mouth, even if it does make me blush as red as a tomato.

"You like that. I can tell. I can feel your pussy soaking my cock, Liv. If I could stay buried inside you forever, it wouldn't be long enough. This pussy is mine."

I find myself falling over the edge. My whole body shakes with the explosive orgasm. Romeo's hands grip my waist, holding me still as he follows me over that edge, emptying himself inside me. I collapse onto him. My head rests on his chest as we both catch our breaths.

"I need to learn how to tattoo," he says, out of the blue.

"Why?" I ask him.

"I want to tattoo my name on the lips of your pussy."

I look at him with widened eyes. "That is never happening."

"Never say never. I can be very persuasive, babe," he says with a smirk.

"I will never be persuaded to let you do that to me, Romeo."

I wake up to an empty bed. Stretching my arms above my head, I smile at the memory of last night's activities. When I asked Romeo to make love to me, I wasn't a hundred percent sure I could do it. I wanted to, but wanting to do something and being able to follow through without panicking are two different things.

Climbing out of bed, I head into the adjoining

bathroom and turn on the hot water. I make quick work of showering and dressing. I brush my hair out before I go in search of Romeo. My face lights up when I enter the living room and find Izzy sitting on the sofa, scowling at her phone.

"Hey, I didn't know you were coming today," I greet her.

"Oh, yeah, me neither." She smiles back at me; however, it's strained.

"What's wrong? Where's Romeo?" I look around the open space, moving towards the kitchen and dining room area.

"He had to step out for a bit. You're stuck with me for a few hours."

"What happened?" I ask her.

"Ah, Savvy is missing."

Savvy is Romeo's brother's new wife. "What do you mean missing?"

"Look, I think you need to ask Romeo when he gets back."

As much as I want to press her for more information, I don't. I get the feeling that no matter how much I push her, she won't tell me anything anyway. "Is Romeo okay?" I ask the one burning question I have. "I mean, crap. It's horrible, beyond awful, that Savvy is missing. I don't mean... I just... crap. I don't know what I mean. I just need to know that he's okay. I'm a terrible person." I sigh. A women is missing, and here I am, worried about my boyfriend. *Fiancé.*

"He's fine, Livvy, and trust me when I say you are far from a horrible person. I've met plenty of truly horrendous people in my lifetime, and you are a fucking saint," Izzy says.

"Thank you." I sit next to her on the sofa. "I'm sorry you got stuck with babysitting duties," I tell her.

"Hey, there is nowhere else I'd rather be. You happen to be my new favorite Valentino." She laughs.

"I'm not a Valentino."

"*Yet*. But you will be."

My phone lights up with an incoming text. I open it without thinking and read the contents.

UNKNOWN:

> You're on borrowed time. Enjoy it while it lasts. They weren't supposed to let you live. I paid to get you out of the picture. I guess you have to do some things yourself.

My hands shake as I reread the message. Izzy snatches the phone from me and frowns at the screen. "Who the fuck sent you this?" she yells.

"I don't know." I'm trying to keep the tears at bay. I'm doing my best not to panic. It takes a moment for my brain to register that Izzy is walking down the hall. I jump up and follow her into Luca's room. Sitting on the bed, Izzy cracks open his laptop and starts typing. "What are you doing?" I ask her.

She glances up at me. "Who's Samantha June?" she asks.

I roll my eyes. "Some cheerleader who wants Romeo. Why?"

"She's not too bright. Idiot sent that message from her own phone."

"Wait... she knows. She said they weren't supposed to leave me alive. How does she know...?"

"Livvy, get dressed. We're going out, and you're getting initiated into the family."

Chapter Twenty-Nine

Romeo

hree days later

They found Savvy. It's been three fucking days of looking for her. I haven't seen Livvy for three fucking days. She's been with Izzy, so I know she's safe and we've spoken on the phone a little. But mostly I've been combing the streets, trying to get any word, any intel on where the fuck Savvy's been. No one knows a thing. Not a single fucking soul. The only detail that came to light was that Petrov ordered Matteo's house burnt to the ground.

Apparently, the fucker I dumped at the hospital as a parting gift woke up. His tongue might not have worked but his fucking hands did, and he typed out the message I left for them.

I killed Dmitri. Petrov is out for blood. Blood he won't get out of me or any of my family. I'm about to make sure of it. Now that I know Savvy is safe, I'm going to finish the job I should have completed weeks ago. I'm sitting out front of the café the Petrovs frequent. I've been here for hours. I was in and out in thirty minutes. The whole place is set to blow.

Just as soon as the fuckers walk in and get settled.

Once I see their cars maneuver onto the street, I turn out of my parking spot and drive around the corner. I pull up the café's camera feed on my laptop. The Russians strut inside and sit at the table in the back. Just like I expected them to. Two stand guard at the door. I don't hesitate before I press the button on my phone. The screen on my laptop goes black as the noise from the explosion deafens the streets. And I drive away with a satisfied smile. I just rid the fucking earth of scum. It's a good fucking feeling. Now I can go home to Livvy.

Just as I'm pulling into the underground garage, my father's name lights up my phone.

"Pops, how you doing?"

"Romeo, what happened to coming to me first before you went rogue?" he says in greeting.

Shit, he knows I just blew the whole Petrov family tree to smithereens. "I knew you'd tell me no. Forgiveness is easier to ask for than permission. You taught me that, remember?"

"Don't use my own words on me, son. What you did was dangerous."

"They fucking raped my girlfriend, Pops. Did you really think I wasn't going to put an end to them?"

"No, I didn't. What I thought was that you'd let me fucking help you." He sighs. "Bring Livvy to Sunday dinner this weekend. I think it's about time we meet the girl who's got you all twisted up."

"Sure. But, just so you know, I'm marrying her, Pops. Don't fucking scare her off."

"She's dating *you*, Romeo. If she ain't scared by now, I doubt much else will send her running." He laughs.

"*Funny.*" I exaggerate the word. "I'll see you Sunday." Hanging up the phone, I walk into the elevator and hit the penthouse button. I need to see my girl. It's been too fucking long. When I walk into the apartment, I find Izzy and Livvy on the sofa watching some rom-com.

"Romeo!" Livvy squeals, jumping up and running at me. I catch her when she throws her arms around my neck, holding her up as she wraps her legs around my waist and slams her lips down on mine. This is a greeting I could get used to coming home to. "Don't ever leave me for that long again," she says between kisses.

"Are you okay?" I ask her, pulling back and letting my eyes take in as much of her face as I can.

"I'm okay," she says.

"I'm sorry I had shit to do."

"All right, kids, I'm heading out. Romeo, call me," Izzy says, passing us on her way to the foyer.

"So what'd you get up to while I was gone?" I ask Livvy, sitting on the sofa with her in my lap.

"I, uh... not much really."

"What aren't you telling me?"

"I got a message. It was from Samantha. Izzy saw it and took me to confront her."

"Confront who?"

"Samantha?"

"Why?"

"She said she paid those men to..." She lets her sentence trail off. She doesn't need to finish it.

"She what? I'm going to fucking kill the bitch."

"That might be hard," Livvy says.

"Why?"

"Because, by the time we got to her place, Samantha was already... she was hanging from a ceiling fan in the middle of her living room."

"She killed herself?" I ask, my brows furrowed.

"Yes."

That doesn't seem right. A girl like that *does not*

kill herself. Then I remember Izzy's words. *"Romeo, call me."* My cousin knows something that she didn't tell Livvy. "I'm sorry you had to see that, babe." I kiss her gently.

"I think I'm a terrible person, Romeo," she whispers.

"Why on earth would you think that? You're the best fucking person I know."

"I'm not. When I saw her, Samantha, I was relieved. I thought, well, at least she can't bother us anymore. That's a horrible thing to think when someone has died."

"You're not a terrible person. You're human."

"That's not all, though. She said she paid those men to kill me. What if they come back? What if they try to finish their job?" she asks, and her voice quivers.

"That's not going to happen," I tell her.

"You don't know that. They said... He said, *'Next time, it's my turn.'* That means they're planning a next time."

"Is this why you haven't wanted to leave the apartment?" I know I haven't exactly pushed her to socialize. I thought she just needed time. I didn't know she thought they were out there looking for her.

"I don't know," she says. "Partly."

"Livvy, those men can't come back for you. I guarantee you that will never happen."

"How can you know that?"

"Because I killed them. Both of them," I admit. I

wait to see the disgust, the loathing in her eyes. The disappointment that I did the one thing she asked me not to do. I can live with her hate if my words, my actions, give her the peace of mind she so desperately needs. "Say something," I beg her. Her silence is killing me.

"I'm sorry you had to do that," she says.

"Olivia, I love you. I will always do whatever has to be done to protect you, to protect us," I tell her. "I need to know that this is something you can live with, Livvy. The knowledge that I've taken lives, that there is no redeeming of whatever soul you think I have."

"Romeo, you have a soul. Do you know how I know?"

"How?"

"Because it's the other half of mine. Because good or bad, I love you, Romeo. I don't want you to have to do those things because of me, but I would never look at you differently for being who you are."

"I'm going to need you to keep that promise, because Pops wants you at Sunday dinner this weekend."

Livvy's eyes open in horror. I just told her that I killed people, that I will again, and the thought of coming to my parents' house for dinner is what scares her?

"What if they don't like me?"

"I'll shoot them." I laugh. "Relax, babe. There is nothing about you that is unlikeable."

"That's not true. There's plenty."

"Like what? Name one thing?"

"I never share the last cookie," she says.

"What? No way. That's a deal breaker, babe. Sorry. How did I not know you were such a terrible person?" I screw up my face in mock disgust.

"See? Not as perfect as you seem to think."

"You are perfect. And I'll always leave the last cookie for you. To eat all by yourself."

"You say the sweetest things, Romeo." She smiles. I fucking live to see that smile.

* * *

As soon as Livvy is asleep, I slide out of bed and call my cousin. "Took you long enough," she answers.

"What the fuck happened, Izzy?"

"That little bitch Samantha *Something* paid those Petrovs to attack Livvy."

"How certain are you?"

"I saw the bank transactions, Romeo. I'm not an amateur," she hisses at me.

"How did Samantha end up swinging from a ceiling fan?" I ask her.

"Well, I was planning on doing the job myself, but then I thought I couldn't really subject Livvy to that. She's far to innocent. So I had one of the boys do it and make it look like a suicide."

"Why would you show her that? She didn't need to see that shit," I yell into the receiver.

"Yes, she did. She needed closure. She needed to know that the nightmare has ended."

"Will it ever really be gone, though? Her nightmare? She still wakes up screaming most nights, Iz."

"I know. I was there. It will take time, Romeo. Just keep doing whatever you're doing, because that girl is crazy about you."

"I'm a lovable person, Iz," I tell her, and she laughs.

"Yep, you are. I gotta go. Talk later." The line cuts out before I get the chance to say goodbye. Or thank you...

Chapter Thirty

Livvy

Livvy

I wipe my sweaty hands down the sides of my coat. I can't stop fidgeting. I don't recall ever being so nervous over anything.

"You look beautiful," Romeo says for the millionth time. "You are going to be fine. I'm right here."

"I know. I'm sorry. I just really want your family to like me."

"Well, you'll know if they don't. Because you'll end up with cement shoes at the bottom of the river."

She gasps. Her mouth hangs open.

"Sorry, bad mafia joke." I laugh.

Livvy tilts her head. "We've never actually had that conversation. Is this your way of confirming that the rumors are true? That your family really is part of the mafia?"

"Babe, you're smart enough to know the answer without us having that conversation," Romeo says.

I nod my head. I think I always knew there was something different about Romeo. I knew he was dangerous. Lethal. I also know that I love him anyway. "Okay, let's do this." I shrug my shoulders. We've been standing at the front door of his childhood home for a few minutes now. "No, wait! I just want to say that I'm sorry. If I screw this up or something, I'm sorry in advance."

"Livvy, there is nothing you can say that will screw this up," he assures me. "Actually, on second thought, let's leave out the fact that your father's a cop and you plan on becoming a district attorney." He winks.

"I'm changing specialties. I want to do family law."

"When did you decide that?"

"A few weeks ago. I've had a change of heart on how justice is served," I tell him.

"Mmm, okay. Come on, let's go before Theo eats everything."

I follow him into the massive home. This is

certainly not anything like how I grew up. This place exudes elegance. Money. I wonder what Romeo will think when I do take him to meet my family, who've been on my case to come home since Christmas.

"Mom?" Romeo calls out.

"In here." A feminine voice calls back, in an Australian accent, and I automatically smile. I remember Romeo mentioning that his mom is Australian. I don't know what it is about that accent, but I just love hearing it.

"Hey, this is Livvy. Livvy, my mom, Holly." Romeo leans in and kisses his mom on the cheek.

"Hello, Mrs. Valentino, it's a pleasure to meet you," I greet her.

"Call me Holly. And welcome, sweetheart. I'm so excited that you're here. Come on, all the girls are out back." Holly takes my hand and leads me towards a hallway. I glance at Romeo, who is following behind me. "Romeo, your dad is in the den," his mom says, without looking at him.

"Ah, yeah, I'll say hello to everyone else first," Romeo replies.

Holly halts midstep. "Romeo Luca Valentino. What on earth do you think I'm going to do with her?" His mother's hand rests on her hip.

"Nothing, Ma. I just want to see my sisters-in-law."

"Bullshit." Holly laughs. "I know you, kid. Now, go see your father and brothers. Dinner will be ready in fifteen."

Romeo looks to me. I know if I give him any indication that I need him right now, he'll stay with me no matter what anyone says. I don't want to come across as that needy. Even if I am. So, instead of begging him not to leave my side, I smile and nod my head slightly, pretending that I'm fine.

Romeo leans in to me. "I know that you're pretending to be fine. I don't fucking like it. Yell out if you need me. The walls in this house are surprisingly thin. I'll hear you," he says, kissing my forehead.

"Thank you."

I turn back to look at Holly, who has unshed tears in her eyes. "I'm sorry. I'm just so happy he found you, sweetie."

"You and me both." I smile and Holly laughs.

After introducing me to Maddie, Lilah, and Savannah, Holly sits next to me at the small kitchen table everyone is gathered around and pulls out her phone. She video-calls someone and then places the screen in front of me on the table. "See, I told you she's real," Holly says to someone I can only assume is her twin sister. Romeo's told me as much as he can about his family. There's a lot of them to remember, but it's pretty obvious by the mirror image of his mother that the lady on the phone is his Aunt Reilly.

"Oh, she's beautiful. Did he kidnap her? How did Romeo manage to tie that one down?" the woman asks. My brows furrow. Are they seriously talking bad about Romeo right now? I don't know if it's family banter or not. It has to be. "I'm sorry, Livvy. It's just that you're way out of his league," the woman continues.

"I'm really not. Romeo is... everything," I say with a smile.

"Oh no, you've been bitten by that Valentino venom." She laughs. "I'm Aunt Reilly, by the way."

"What's the Valentino venom?" I ask.

"All you girls sitting at that table are suffering from it," she says.

"Ah, nope, not me," Maddie's sister yells out.

"Well, everyone but Lilah," Reilly clarifies.

"Don't listen to her, Livvy. She's the crazy twin. She thinks the Valentino men have some kind of poison they use to keep us addicted to them." Holly rolls her eyes.

"Oh, well, I don't want the antidote if that's true. I'll live in ignorant bliss," I say with a grin.

* * *

I'm absolutely stuffed. Dinner was amazing. Romeo's family is great. I'm not sure why I was so scared to meet them. I'm not really seeing what's so terrifying about his dad either. I get that he's supposed to be this big scary mob boss, but all I've seen is a doting husband and a loving father. He loves his family and he's welcomed me in with open arms.

His exact words were: "I couldn't have asked for a

better match for my son, and I can't wait to tell the world that you're my new daughter-in-law."

I do think they get a bit carried away with the whole marriage thing. I might have said yes to Romeo, but that was with the stipulation that we wait until after graduation.

"Thanks for dinner, Ma. We have to go." Romeo stands. Taking my hand, he pulls me up with him.

"You haven't had dessert yet," Holly says.

"I'm stuffed, and we both have studying to do."

"Romeo, I thought we were done pretending you were stupid and needed to actually study?" This comes from his brother, Matteo.

"Savannah, hit him for me," Romeo asks Matteo's wife, who reaches behind her husband and slaps his head.

"Ouch. What was that for?" he whines.

"Leave them alone, Tao. Look how cute they are." She sighs, her eyes flicking from me to Romeo.

"Livvy is cute. *He's* fucking ugly. Every family has one you know. An ugly duckling," Matteo says.

"Okay, on that note, we'll see you next week, Ma. Pops, thank you." Romeo hugs and kisses both of his parents. They stand, and Holly pulls me into a hug, telling me how excited she is that I came. When Mr. Valentino approaches me next, I freeze.

Please don't hug me, please don't hug me, please don't hug me. I'm begging him internally.

Romeo notices. Of course he does. He steps ever so

slightly in front of me. His dad stops and looks at us. "Livvy, it was a pleasure meeting you. Our home is your home. You're always welcome here," Mr. Valentino says.

"Thank you." My voice is quiet. I feel like everyone is watching me. The broken girl who needs her fiancé to be her shield. I'm sure they can all see it. I feel so stupid. I was doing so well, right up until I thought his dad was going to embrace me. Once we're closed inside the car, I let the tears I was holding in fall. "I'm so sorry," I tell Romeo.

"Shit, Livvy. Come here." Romeo pulls me over the center console. I straddle his lap as he shifts the driver's seat backwards, creating more room. "You're okay. You're okay," he whispers, cupping my face with his palms.

"I don't know what happened. I didn't mean to. I just..."

"Stop, you don't need to explain anything. I get it. I will always be there to help you through any situation."

"It's not normal, Romeo. I should be able to let your dad hug me." I sniffle.

"And you will, when you're ready to, and not a fucking minute before. What you went through, Livvy, that's not going to go away overnight. It will take time. It's okay."

"They're going to think I'm rude, or clingy, or... I don't know," I cry.

"No, they're not. They love you. But it doesn't

247

matter what they think, because I love you. That's all that matters. You and me."

"I love you. I just want to be the kind of fiancée you can be proud of," I tell him.

"Say it again?"

"What?"

"Fiancée. I like hearing you say it."

"You, Romeo Luca Valentino, are my fiancé. I'm going to marry you. I'm going to have your babies. We're going to live happily ever after."

"Yes, we are."

"Well, that's if my dad doesn't kill you first. You still have to meet my family, you know."

"Let's go this week."

"Where?"

"To Covington. To meet your family."

"What if they can tell what happened to me?"

"They love you, Livvy. They will want to help you. That's all."

"They'll want to move me back to Covington. They'll want to wrap me in cotton wool and never let me leave the house. You don't know them like I do."

"I think I'm going to get along just fine with them, because that is exactly what I want to do with you. Wrap you up in cotton wool and never let you leave my sight."

"Could there be finer symptoms? Is not general incivility the very essence of love?" I quote Jane Austen.

"You have bewitched me body and soul, and I love you," Romeo responds with the famous words of Mr. Darcy.

"You know, I used to think I wanted a real-life version of Romeo or Darcy. But I got better. Because I got both," I say, leaning in and kissing him.

"Let's go home before they realize we haven't left yet," Romeo says, pulling back from our kiss.

"Thank you for being so perfectly you. I don't know what I'd do without you, Romeo."

"Well, it's a good thing you'll never have to find out. Because I will always be here."

As he drives us to his apartment, I look up into the night skies and thank whatever god is listening for sending me Romeo. I will be forever grateful for his love. His heart is something I will always cherish.

Epilogue

Romeo

Four years later

If you'd asked me four years ago if I'd be attending my twin brother's first pro football game with my wife and six-month-old daughter, I would have laughed in your face and asked what drugs you were on. And why you weren't sharing them with me.

As I watch Livvy chat with my mom, who is monopolizing my daughter, Matilda, I can't help but grin. The whole family is here. Sitting in the private box Pops bought for the season.

"What do you think the chances are of your mother handing over my granddaughter?" Pops asks from beside me, staring in the same direction I am.

"Slim to none. She's my daughter and I can't even get her back." I laugh.

"I'm going in. Wish me luck," Pops says, crossing the room to where Livvy and Mom are standing with Maddie and Savannah.

"A hundred says he flops." Matteo pulls out a one-hundred-dollar bill.

"You're on," I say, matching his bet.

We watch as Pops whispers something in Mom's ear. Theo, Matteo, and I all cringe and look away, cursing under our breaths. Whatever he said, I don't want to know. It worked though, because when I turn back around, Mom is handing Matilda over to my dad with a smirk on her face. Pops pivots with Matilda in his arms, and a triumphant smile spreads across his lips —you'd think the man just won the fucking lottery.

"Oh, T, FYI... Matilda needs changing. The diaper bag is over there." Mom points to the huge-as-fuck bag I have to cart around with all of my daughter's things. Babies require a lot of shit. Who would have known such a sweet little girl would need so much crap?

"It's cool. I got this," Pops says.

I walk over, ready to step in and change my daughter myself. "Want me to do that?" I ask my old man as he lays Matilda down on the makeshift changing table.

"I've had four kids, Romeo. You really think I don't know how to change a diaper?" he grunts at me.

"Well, considering I've never seen you change one...? Yeah, I have my doubts." I laugh.

He doesn't respond as he digs through the bag and pulls out the diaper, wipes, and powder. "All right, Tilly, Nonno has this covered." I watch with hawk-like eyes as my dad changes Matilda. He's obviously done this before. Once he's finished, he picks her up again. "And they all doubted me, fuckers," Pops says to Matilda. To which, she grins in response.

"I swear to God if her first word is *fuckers*, I'm shooting you," I groan at my dad.

"Please, we all know her first word will be *Nonno*." He kisses Matilda's forehead. "I have a good feeling about this one," he adds, looking down at her.

My dad has been trying to get all of his grandchildren's first words to be *Nonno*. Between Theo and Matteo, he's already lucked out four times. I think my brothers are in competition with each other to see who can knock their wife up the most. Theo and Maddie have Liliana, who's three. And Alessandro, who's one. Matteo and Savvy have two boys: Lorenzo, who just turned two, and Enzo, who's one month older than Matilda. The good thing about my older brothers bringing all these children into the world is that my daughter will have plenty of cousins to keep little shits away from her.

My phone vibrates in my pocket. Pulling it out, I frown when I see Luca's name flash across the screen. "I'll be right back," I tell whomever's listening and step out of the box. "Pretty sure you're supposed to be getting ready for a pretty important game, Luc," I answer.

"Yeah, I was born ready for this shit. Is everyone here?" he asks.

"Yep, waiting for the star of the family to run out onto the field."

"I have a bad feeling, Romeo. Like, something's off."

"It's probably nerves. Everything's fine," I try to convince him, even though I've had that gut feeling for the past hour too. I put it down to me picking up on my twin's pregame nerves.

"Did you bring Matilda?"

"Of course. She's not missing her uncle's claim to fame."

"I think you should send her and Livvy home. Something isn't right, Romeo."

"We're in a secluded box with Pops, Theo, Matteo, Uncle Neo, and Aunt Angelica. What the fuck do you think is going to happen?" I ask him.

"I don't know. You're probably right. I gotta go. Just, if anything happens, you get them out of here."

"Luca, that's my wife and daughter. You really think I wouldn't get them out at the first sign of trouble?"

"I think you'd try to save everyone, Romeo, and I just want you to know... if it did ever come down to it, if you had to choose between me or them, always choose them."

"That will never happen," I grunt. I don't like where he's taking this conversation. I fucking hate talking about this shit. Livvy and Matilda will always come first to me, but my family... I'll never let them go either.

"Okay, I gotta go."

"Talk to you at halftime," I say, cutting the call and walking back into the room with the weight of the fucking world on my shoulders.

Livvy

Romeo walks back into the room, and straightaway I can tell something's wrong. My eyes follow him to the wet bar, watching as he downs a glass of whiskey.

"I'll be back." I excuse myself from Holly, who has to be the world's best mother-in-law. I mean, I haven't had any others and never plan to, but to say I'm a little in love with Holly Valentino is an understatement. "Everything okay? And don't try to lie to me and tell me it is."

Romeo turns to look at me, his arm wraps around the back of my shoulders, and he pulls me into my favorite place in the whole world. His arms. My face rests against his chest. "Luca is nervous that something's wrong," he says.

"Okay, what do you think?" I ask him.

"I thought it was just his pregame nerves. But what if something _is_ wrong? What if I've brought you and Matilda here and it's not safe?" His words are softly spoken into my ear.

"Look around, Romeo. We're surrounded by your family. We couldn't be safer."

"You could be at home," he says.

"Romeo, you and Luca really need to get your shit together. You can't stop Matilda from entering the world. I hate to break it to you, but she will grow up. She will have friends. She'll even go to sleepovers at other people's places. She's a kid, so let her be one."

"She's a fucking princess. And, as for sleepovers, that's never fucking happening. Ever," he grunts.

I laugh. I love that he's protective. He just goes a little overboard sometimes. "Look, if something happens, I have faith that you, your brothers, and your dad will handle it and get us all out in one piece."

Romeo inhales and exhales before he releases me from his arms. "You're right."

"Haven't you heard?" I ask him.

"What?"

"I'm always right." I smile.

Romeo laughs and tugs me towards where his brothers are crowded at the window. His dad is still cuddling with Matilda over on the sofa with Holly, who's trying to get another turn at holding her grandbaby.

"Game's about to start," Romeo hollers out to everyone. The whole family stands against the window, watching the game below. We all cheer and roar as Luca runs onto the field. I'm so freaking proud of him. He set out to achieve this dream and he did it.

"Wait, Kat Star is singing the anthem?" Savannah squeals in excitement.

"No way!" I say, shoving my face closer to the window.

"Why didn't anyone tell us?" Maddie asks.

"Ah, because you're all fucking crazy." This comes from Uncle Neo. My father-in-law reaches out and slaps him across the head. "Ow, what the fuck, T?"

"Don't call my daughters crazy," he grunts.

"If the shoe fits..." Neo says, sidestepping another slap.

"Okay, shhh, she's about to start singing," I tell them.

Luca

Something's not right. I know Romeo insists it's just my usual pregame jitters, but that's not it. I know what pre-game jitters are. This feeling in the pit of my stomach is not nerves. It's dread. Something is going to go down. I just fucking wish I knew what it was.

Standing here, in line with my teammates for my first professional game, I should be pumped. Instead, I'm scanning the field, the crowd, the makeshift platform stage right in front of me. That's when I see it. A red beam in the center of the singer's chest. Without thought, I charge forward. It takes me three seconds to reach the girl and tackle her to the ground. I cover her body with my own. Ten more seconds, and we're surrounded by security while people yell and pull at me.

My gaze is locked on the caramel-honey eyes belonging to the woman currently beneath my much larger frame. She has me in some sort of trance. I can't tear my focus away. Until a sharp pain radiates through my side when two big security guards roll me off her.

I've been shot. It's not the first time I've had a bullet rip through my body—fucking hurts like a motherfucker though. However, when my head drops to the side and I see her face, I know it was worth it. "In case I die today, you should know you're really fucking beautiful," I tell her.

"Thank you, but you're not dying. I can't live with that kind of guilt, so you'll just have to suck it up and live." She smiles.

Romeo

I run. The second I see Luca race from his spot on the field, I ran out the door.

"Neo, get the girls out of here," I yell as I exit the room. I can hear footsteps following me, I don't look back though. I feel it. The moment my brother is hit, I get a sharp pain in the right side of my body. "Fuck, he's been shot!" I say, turning around to see my dad, Theo, and Matteo all crowded behind me.

I run faster. I need to get to him. He's fucking out there alone. He should never be alone. I push through the throngs of people who are rushing for the exit. We're the only ones running towards the field. It's utter chaos. I get to the stage just as Luca is being pulled up on a stretcher.

"Luc, bro, you good?" I ask him.

"I met an angel," he says with a lopsided grin.

"Fuck, no fucking angels, Luca. You're destined for hell, remember? We've got our own apartment on layaway there." My eyes scan his body. He seems okay. The medics are cutting his clothes and padding off.

"I'm fine, Romeo. It's just a little bullet hole. I need you to get her out of here. That bullet was meant for her," he says.

"Who?" I ask. He nods his head to one side and I follow the direction, spotting the singer Livvy is obsessed with. The girl's surrounded by security. She's yelling about something, trying to get past them. "I've got her."

"Get the footage from every goddamn camera in this place. One of them has to have seen something," Pops says to Theo and Matteo.

"I think she wants you to move, assholes." I grab one of the security guys from the back of his shirt and shove him away from the woman. "Need a hand, sweetheart?" I ask her.

"Thank you." She barges past me, falling to the ground next to Luca. "I'm Katarina. We didn't get to meet properly," she says.

"Luca."

I watch, knowing all too well the look in my twin brother's eyes. He's just caught the one thing he swore he never would. *Feelings for a woman.*

"Do me a favor. Let my brothers get you out of here," he says.

"Are you going to be okay? Why isn't there an ambulance here yet?" Katarina yells out, looking around the stadium.

"I'm fine. This is nothing. Just a scratch." Luca smirks.

"Come on, let's go." I pull the girl to her feet.

"Romeo..." Luca starts, then stops whatever he was about to say.

"I know, man. I know," I tell him. Because I do. I know better than anyone...

Do you still need more of Romeo & Livvy? Get your hands on their bonus scene here - When Romeo meets Livvy's parents.

Acknowledgments

Thank you to everyone that has read Romeo and Livvy's story. You guys are what keep me going!!

I'd like to thank my Patron members, who continue to keep my spirits lifted with their faith and belief in my words. Tawny, Shawna, Megan, Penny, Lauren, Krystle, Gemma, Erin, Edna, Ashley, Melissa, Rhonda, Kim, Juliet, Jenna, Monique, Kayla, Sam, Chris, Amber and Michelle. Thank you, thank you thank you for everything!!

My beta readers, Vicki, Amy, Melissa and Sam, you are all priceless. Romeo and Livvy's journey would not be the same without you.

My content designer Assunta, you are an absolute gem!! Without you, not half as many people would know the Valentino Sons, thank you for the amazing content and keeping my socials looking as fab as they do!

My editor, Kat, the one who polishes the story to make it the best it can possibly be. I could not do this without her—if I could lock her in my basement and keep her editing for me only, for the rest of her days, I would! Maybe I should ask Matteo to arrange this for me.

I have to thank Sammi B, from Sammi Bee Designs, the amazingly talented cover designer, who worked tirelessly on the beautiful covers for the Sons of Valentino Series.

About Kylie Kent

Kylie is a hopeless romantic with a little bit of a dark and twisted side. She loves love, no matter what form it comes in. Sweat, psychotic, stalkerish it doesn't matter as long as the story ends in a happy ending and tons of built in spice.

There is nothing she loves doing more than getting lost in a fictional world, going on adventures that only stories can take you.

Kylie loves to hear from her readers; you can reach her at: author.kylie.kent@gmail.com

For a complete reading order visit

Visit Kylie's website : www.kyliekent.com

Made in United States
Orlando, FL
26 June 2024

48322903R00157